Tennessee River

Cafe

A Short Story Collection

Beth Curtis

𝕮𝔣𝔭

Caney Fork Press

Cover Photograph: ID 21435137 © Eric Hinson Dreamstime.com

CFP

Caney Fork Press For more information contact at:
www.caneyforkpress.com

ISBN-10: 069245991X

ISBN-13: 978-0-692-45991-1

DEDICATION

For my parents, whose support made this book possible.
For my big extended family,
some of the best storytellers I know.

CONTENTS

MISS RUBY

"Oh, hey, Miss Ruby," Anna Grace greeted her customer as she came through the door, the bell on the door tinkling as it closed. "I'll be right with you. Let me just get these plates back to the kitchen." Anna Grace carried a load of plates through the diner and into the kitchen in the back. When she came back, Miss Ruby was still standing up front. Anna Grace watched as the meager, boney, little bit of a woman lifted her nose up in the air a little to scan the room with her usual scowl, daring anyone to speak to her. Deputy Mankin and Sheriff McCord were the only customers that late in the morning. McCord came down from Farrington, the county seat, once a week to check on things with Deputy Mankin. They paid no attention to Ruby. Anna Grace grabbed the coffee pot as she passed by the coffee station, and offered the men more coffee.

"No, honey, we're gettin' ready to head out," Sheriff McCord said.

Anna Grace returned the coffee pot and walked behind the checkout counter up front. "Alright, Miss Ruby," she said as she reached for a pack of cigarettes, "will that be all today?"

Ruby peeked over her shoulder toward the men, and said nothing. The men were making their way up to the counter. Ruby looked down behind her at their boots. She stepped back into the room and looked the other way.

"Okay, gentlemen," Anna Grace said as she accepted their money and dropped it in the register. "Ya'll have a nice day." The men put on their hats and left.

Ruby stepped back up to the counter and held out some crumpled up bills and coins. Anna Grace counted out thirty-five cents to pay for the cigarettes.

"Thank you, Miss Ruby," she said, looking at the withered up woman, letting time pass in case she had something to say. "You okay, Miss Ruby?" Ruby turned abruptly and left, leaving the bell tinkling behind her.

Anna Grace began to clear the table where the men had been sitting, but her thoughts were on Ruby. It was normal for Ruby to be brusque, but it seemed that there was something on her mind today. Oh well, she would be back in tomorrow. Maybe she would say something then.

Anna Grace spent her summers with her great aunts working in their diner, the Tennessee River Cafe. Aunt Ed and Aunt Sally had saved up their money and with a little help from their brothers, purchased the cafe, and had been serving folks there for the past thirty-five years. The two sisters lived two houses down in a large rambling house that faced the river. Early each morning, Anna Grace and her Aunt Sally walked over to the cafe. Aunt Sally got the biscuits going, while Anna Grace opened the curtains, took down the chairs, and started the coffee. Aunt Ed would come along directly, after she straightened up from their breakfast out on the back porch.

Business was brisk at the little cafe at the corner of Main and River Road. The front looked out to the hotel across Main and the side windows gave a view of the Tennessee River and the ferry landing down at the bottom of the hill. Customers came from the hotel, the two factories, the flag factory and the sock factory, or the sawmill. And this summer there was a big highway department road project going on. Most every morning men were waiting for the doors to open for breakfast.

But things really got crazy when a barge pulled in. Barges pulled in at the ferry landing to drop off and pick up crew who worked twenty-one days on and fourteen days off. And sometimes they let the whole crew off to eat and have some free time onshore. As soon as Anna Grace saw a barge pulling in, she knew there wasn't much time to get ready.

Anna Grace wiped down the table, walked back to the kitchen, and put the plates in the large soaker pan in the sink.

"Really, Anna Grace, you shouldn't encourage that ol' woman," Aunt Sally spoke up from her stool as she peeled potatoes for the lunch crowd, her gnarled fingers moving the paring knife through the potato, leaving a curl of skin behind.

"I think she's interesting." Anna Grace reached for a piece of potato, but her aunt smacked her hand back. "I've never met anyone like her."

"There's a reason for that," Aunt Sally said as she wiped her forehead with the back of her hand.

"I sure can't think of anything that would be interesting about that old woman, green teeth, and I bet she wouldn't weigh more than ninety pounds soakin' wet. Just a bit of white trash," Aunt Ed spoke up, as she was finishing off the cornbread batter. Aunt Ed's real name was Edna, but the family always called her Ed or Aunt Ed. Anna Grace wasn't sure how that got started, but she suspected it was left over from a childhood with lots of brothers. "Just a mean, hateful ol' woman. Nothing interesting there, sashaying around in those men's trousers." Aunt Ed pulled the cast iron skillet out of the oven and poured the hot grease into the batter. The batter sizzled.

Ruby had told Anna Grace that when her clothes gave out, "I just took to wearing Pappy's clothes since he wouldn't be needin 'em no more. He done passed a while back."

"Her father was a shiner," Aunt Ed continued as she put the skillet on the stove and stirred the batter, "had a small patch of burley at the front of their holler."

"He was a wiry, ol' muskrat looking man, lived back in that holler," Mary Nell spoke up from washing dishes at the sink. Mary Nell was about nineteen and she'd been working at the cafe for the past several years, washing dishes, doing some prep work in the kitchen, and she helped Anna Grace out front when it got busy. "Least that's what my granny says," she explained. "Lost his wife to some sickness. Left him with them two girls to raise back in that holler. Ruby and her sister."

"Ruby has a sister?" Anna Grace asked.

"No," Aunt Ed said as she dumped beans into a pot on the stove. "The woman died of cancer about ten years ago or so, wouldn't you say Sally?"

"Yes, that'd be about right," Aunt Sally answered. "Her husband moved on after that, never seen around here again."

"Yeah, and that daughter of theirs, Jolene was her name, took up with one of them men on the crew puttin' in the water and sewer lines. Just up and left town with him when the job was done," Mary Nell added. "Though I heard she's been back in town lately."

"Did you know that Miss Ruby has never been more than five miles from here?" Anna Grace asked, popping a piece of potato in her mouth before her aunt could smack her hand. "She says that's just about as far as she ever cared to walk. Except for the time when she was young and snuck onto a barge and they had to put her on another barge to bring her back home."

"Yeah, there was a big scandal 'bout that." Mary Nell straightened up from the sink and turned off the water. "I ask't my granny about Ruby one time. I'd been seeing her walkin' all over the place, here and there, walking into town." Mary Nell leaned up against the sink, wiping her hands with a towel. "Granny said they never really knew what persuaded Ruby to get on that barge, but that's where her future husband was. Nobody could tell if she knew him before, or met him on that barge. But, nevertheless, soon as he got back, he married her, her being only fifteen year' old, and him being more than thirty."

"She married at fifteen!" exclaimed Anna Grace. "That's just a year older than me!"

"Now, don't get any ideas, young lady," Aunt Sally warned.

"Yep, but little good that did her." Mary Nell flipped over a crate and sat down. "Granny says he weren't never home much to speak of, left his job on the barge soon after they married, went off and became a railroad man. Left Ruby there with her daddy. Pretty much never came home." Mary Nell swatted at a fly with her towel.

"Mary Nell, we need to get that catfish out, get it soaking," Aunt

Ed called from the stove.

"Yes'um, I'm right on it," Mary Nell replied. She turned back to Anna Grace and hunched down on her crate a little, leaned forward with her arms on her legs, and lowered her voice. "Granny says that when her husband got hisself killed on that railroad, Ruby hadn't even knowed him enough to mourn. No sir, not a speck of tears from her there at his graveside, no children to stand there beside her, or nothin'." Aunt Ed gave an impatient huff from over at the stove. "I'm a'gettin' it, Miss Edna. I'm a' goin'." Mary Nell jumped up from the crate and headed towards the back.

"Well, she only comes in here when you're here, Anna Grace," Aunt Sally said, still peeling potatoes. "So, I say you just don't need to be encouraging her." She stopped peeling and shook her paring knife at Anna Grace, "calling her *Miss* Ruby and all."

"She's my elder."

"Hummph," Aunt Sally snorted.

"I think she just needs somebody to talk to." Anna Grace grabbed up the ketchup and headed for the front to fill bottles. As she worked, she thought of what *she* knew of Miss Ruby from talking to her.

Miss Ruby had not been easy to get to know. She would let out a little at the time, and then when she was done she would just turn and walk out the door, no good-bye, see ya later, or nothing. When Anna Grace would ask her how she was, most times she wouldn't even respond, just jump right into what ever was on her mind. Sometimes, though, she was "fair to middlin'." One day Anna Grace had actually witnessed a smile from her. Miss Ruby had come in for her cigarettes, Pall Malls in the red pack, the only thing she ever purchased.

"Just guess what has happened over to my place," Ruby asked in her short clipped way, moving her long plait of hair over her shoulder and down her back.

"Well, I don't know, Miss Ruby, what happened?" Anna Grace reached for the red pack of cigarettes.

"Now lookey here, you know how I been without 'lectricity and plumbing since I been a'livin' in that trailer of my niece's…"

Ruby had explained to Anna Grace a while back that one day

her niece, Jolene, and her "worthless" husband, Fred, had just showed up out of the blue, and since there were two of them and just one of her, they were going to take the cabin and bring up a nice trailer for Ruby. They were her only surviving kin, Ruby explained, so she tried to be as hospitable as possible. When that old beat-up trailer arrived, "weren't nothin' but a box," it was too late. Jolene and Fred were firmly planted in her home.

"No, Miss Ruby, I had no idea you were living like that. How horrible." Anna Grace waited while Ruby dug around in her pants pocket for her money. Ruby couldn't read or write, and she couldn't count money, so she would just hold out her crumpled up bills and coins for Anna Grace to take what she needed to pay for the cigarettes.

"Well I have." Ruby held her money out in an open hand. Anna Grace took the money for the cigarettes and handed her the pack. "Anyhow," Ruby pushed her hat back off her face a bit, "I had no place to go to the bathroom, so I just been a'walkin' on up to the house to use the bathroom there. It weren't easy at night, but that's what I had." Ruby began packing the cigarettes on the palm of her hand. "You know I have me a fine bathroom, runnin' water and all up at the house?"

"No, I didn't know that, Miss Ruby."

"Yes siree, I do indeed. My Ricky—that was my husband, ever'body called him Muskrat." Ruby let out a little giggle. "Muskrat Wheeler. Yes sir, Muskrat and Ruby Wheeler." She stood, lost for the moment in the past. "Anyhow," Ruby snapped back, "he died a long time ago. Well sir, he came home from the railroad with a passel of money one time, and said he was just dang tired of going outside to do his business, and he didn't take too kindly to taking a bath on the back porch in that big ol' tub we had." Ruby started opening her pack of cigarettes. "So he just up and buys a pump for that spring, and builds us a fine indoors bathroom, and runnin' water in the kitchen to boot. Daddy said it was a sad waste of good money, but," Miss Ruby giggled a little, "boy I tell you, I thought I was somethin'."

Ruby lit a cigarette, inhaled deeply, and pointing the cigarette at Anna Grace, continued. "Anyhow," she said with streams of smoke leaking from her mouth and nose, "now, my niece, Jolene."

She stopped and tried to spit a piece of tobacco off her tongue. "My niece, Jolene, she was none too happy about any of this, what with me coming and going and all, especially when I mentioned wanting to take a bath!" Ruby picked a piece of tobacco from her tongue. "Well, the other morning I woke up to all sorts of noise and men's voices outside my trailer. And," Miss Ruby stood a little taller, a hint of a smile beginning to unfold, "those men put me in a little outhouse out back of the trailer. Then, they brought my big washtub from up to the house, and built me a back porch off 'a the trailer to put it on. And," Miss Ruby paused for dramatic effect, "white boy Larry hooked up me some 'lectricity!"

"That's real nice, Miss Ruby." Anna Grace was wiping down the counter. Ruby took another draw from her cigarette, grinned a little bit with smoke circling her face as she exhaled. Anna Grace kept wiping. "Why do you call him white boy Larry?"

Ruby stubbed out her cigarette in an ashtray on the counter with a little more force than necessary. "Well it weren't black boy Larry what done the job." Ruby grabbed her pack off the counter and turned to leave. Then she turned back to the counter with that scowl on her face again, grabbed two books of complimentary matches, and left, the door bell tinkling after her.

Ruby didn't come in every day. She came in every few days or so, and when she did, she usually came between the breakfast and lunch crowd. Most times there weren't many people in the cafe, if any at all. If it were the first of the month she would go by the bank with her social security check before coming to the cafe.

One particular morning, after being at the bank, she seemed agitated with excitement. "Guess what my check says that comes to me each month?"

"What does it say, Miss Ruby?"

"Well, ya see, I had that teller down there at the bank read it to me. She'd point at each word and told me what it says." Ruby unfolded her body a little and held her chin high. "It says *The United States of America* right there just along the top of my check in big letters, just as pretty as you please. Imagine that. The United States of America, right there." Anna Grace thought she saw the beginning of a grin break across Ruby's face, but then in a flash she was back to scowling. "Yep, my pappy left me some money in that bank, but I don't use it." Ruby moved closer and lowered her voice. "I think it may be ill-gotten money. So I just use the money that The United States of America give me." Ruby gave a short laugh.

"That's pretty swell, Miss Ruby." Anna Grace pulled down the Pall Mall cigarettes from the shelf. "Miss Ruby, why do you come in here to buy your cigarettes? I mean you could buy them at the drug store, or when you get your groceries." Ruby pulled out her money from her pants pocket with that scowl on her face. Anna Grace took the thirty-five cents for the cigarettes from her hand. "Why do you come in here to buy them?" she asked again.

"Just do, that's why," and without another word, Ruby turned and left.

ℰℛ

Anna Grace came back to the present with a start, realizing she was holding a big ketchup bottle and staring out the window at the ornate ironwork on the balcony of the Jamison Hotel. She put the ketchup bottle down and started stocking cigarettes on the shelves behind the counter. She worried about Miss Ruby. She wondered again about her odd, silent behavior this morning. She sure was acting kind of strange, stranger than usual, even for Miss Ruby.

It was another couple of days before Ruby came in the cafe again. When Anna Grace turned at the sound of the bell above the door, and saw Miss Ruby, she became a little concerned again. Ruby was kind of drawn into herself, looking around the room as if to see if anyone were listening. They were alone.

"You okay, Miss Ruby?" Anna Grace asked.

"Now I don't like to be beholden to no one," she looked around again, lowering her voice, "but, if I were to need to talk to someone, maybe someone that knew about all that law stuff, who do you think I should talk to?" Ruby glanced out the door and back to Anna Grace.

"Well, I reckon if I were to say someone, I would say Lawyer Gibbons across the street. Folks seem to like him. He comes in here pretty often." Anna Grace watched Ruby.

"Okay, I'll talk to him," Ruby said.

"His office is right across the street, up over the drug store."

Anna Grace pointed.

"No, you talk to him." Ruby folded her arms across her chest.

"What do you want me to say to him, Miss Ruby?"

"That I need to talk to him." She impatiently looked out the door again.

"Well, alright. Do you want me to go over there with you?"

"No, have him come here. Tomorrow, 'bout this time." Ruby turned to leave.

"Well, okay, Miss Ruby." Anna Grace hesitated as she watched Ruby's back stalk out the door.

∞

Ruby paced around the front of the cafe the next morning, looking out the door, then the windows. Then she spotted something, straightened up her crumpled body and went back to stand at the door. Lawyer Gibbons walked in the door pulling out his handkerchief and mopping his face. Ruby stepped back a few paces. "It's already a muggy one out there." He looked at Anna Grace then at Ruby as he returned his handkerchief to his pocket. "Well, Ruby," he said, removing his hat, "I understand you're wanting to talk with me."

Ruby hesitated. "Yes," was all she could mumble.

"Mornin' Mr. Gibbons," Anna Grace called from behind the counter.

"Hidy there, how you doing this morning, gal?" Gibbons hung his hat on the hat rack and looked around the empty cafe.

"Just fine, thank you," Anna Grace smiled.

Lawyer Gibbons looked back at Ruby. "Ruby, let's go back to a table and see what's on your mind." Ruby followed him back to a table in the rear corner, shuffling along in her daddy's boots that were too big. He didn't hold her chair for her. Anna Grace turned down the radio behind the counter that was blaring the morning farm report. Then she realized that Ruby had never sat down at a table in the cafe before, and she intended to treat her like a customer.

"You all want to order something to drink or eat?" she asked her customers.

"Yes, darlin', I think I will." Gibbons arranged his silverware.

"I think I'll have some late breakfast. Bring me some eggs, ham, biscuits and some gravy. And, keep the coffee coming."

"And you, Miss Ruby, what would you like?" Ruby started digging into her pocket. "No, Miss Ruby it's on me." Anna Grace touched the woman's arm that was searching for money in her pocket. Ruby stopped moving.

"What?"

"It's free, Miss Ruby."

"Oh." She pulled her hand back and rested her hands on the table. "Well then."

"Yes, Miss Ruby." Anna Grace waited for a moment. "What would you like to eat?"

"Well I done had breakfast."

"Would you like some coffee?" Anna Grace asked.

"Yes, coffee. I'll have some coffee," Miss Ruby said.

After Anna Grace had given Mr. Gibbons' order to her aunts in the back, she came back out front and went to the coffee station. She glanced over to the table. There was no talking going on. She looked at Ruby's rigid back facing her, and then caught a glance from Gibbons. Fortunately there were no other customers in the cafe at the time, just the three of them. But that didn't seem to give comfort to Ruby. Anna Grace returned to the table and placed the two coffee cups and saucers down. She lingered for a moment as she poured the coffee. Lawyer Gibbons took up the sugar dispenser and made a show of measuring a level spoonful into his cup.

"Now Ruby, I'm a lawyer." He stirred his coffee and waited. "Is there something you need to talk with me about pertaining to the law?"

Ruby just sat there with her hands clasped on the table, starring into space, back still rigid. Gibbons looked up at Anna Grace. She gave him a glance that pleaded patience.

"Miss Ruby," she said, "you can talk to Lawyer Gibbons about anything you want, and he won't tell anybody what you say. Not even me. It's okay, you can trust him." Ruby continued to stay quiet.

"I tell you what," Gibbons spoke up. "I'm gonna enjoy me a good breakfast, and if you feel so moved, you can just speak your piece when you're ready."

Anna Grace left the table mouthing a "thank you" to Gibbons. She patted Miss Ruby on the shoulder. As far as she could tell, when she served Gibbons his breakfast, there had still been no conversation. Gibbons folded up the newspaper he had been looking over.

"Thank you, darlin'. Could you bring me some hot sauce for my eggs?"

Anna Grace nodded and left. She brought the hot sauce over to the table, and still no talking from Miss Ruby. She went to the back to get the salt and pepper to refill shakers, and when she returned to the front, Ruby was talking. She still had her hands clasped on the table in front of her, not looking directly at Lawyer Gibbons. Anna Grace put the salt and pepper on the front counter, careful not to do anything that might interrupt the quiet flow of words. Ruby continued talking. Anna Grace went outside and sat on the bench out front to give them their privacy, watching, in case she was needed. Lawyer Gibbons would shake his head no, as he was eating, or nod in agreement, but let the woman talk. He finished his breakfast, and Anna Grace went in to the table to get his plate. "Would you like a refill on your coffee, Mr. Gibbons?"

"No, darlin', I'm good." He laid some bills on the table and said, "keep the change." As he stood, he looked down at Ruby. "Ruby, I think we can get all that you want done. You just come on over to the office any time and we'll get it taken care of." He turned to leave.

"I don't see any better time than right now," Ruby spoke quietly.

Gibbons looked at Anna Grace then back to Ruby. "Well, alright. Let's get it done." Ruby stood and followed Gibbons out of the diner never looking at Anna Grace.

80CB

Over the next two summers, Ruby continued coming into the cafe when Anna Grace was there. They continued to have their conversations, never lasting more than a minute or so.

"Miss Ruby, you ever been in a department store?" Anna Grace asked.

"No, but I walk down to the dry goods store ever now and then."

"Miss Ruby, you ever been on an airplane?"

"No, but I seen a few fly overhead."

"Yeah, me too," Anna Grace thought out loud.

"Poke salad is up real nice back in the holler. Had me a mess last night. Caught a big ol' large mouth down at the river to go with 'em. Now, I have my husband's fancy fishing rod and reel. But I just never got the hang of using it. I just still use my cane pole. But I keep that rod and reel hanging on the wall just over my bed."

℘ℛ

The summer after Anna Grace graduated from high school, Lawyer Gibbons came in one morning to inform Anna Grace that Ruby had passed away the night before. He was on his way down to the funeral home to talk to Jolene.

"Can you come by my office tomorrow morning?" Gibbons asked Anna Grace. "Miss Ruby asked for you to be present for the reading of her will."

"Me?" Anna Grace was stunned. "Are you sure?"

Gibbons laughed. "Yes, I'm sure. Can you be there around ten o'clock?"

"Yes, sir."

After Lawyer Gibbons left, Anna Grace sat down at one of the tables. Images of Miss Ruby swirled through her head. She would certainly miss the little old woman. But she sure left her with memories that made her smile.

"Aunt Sally..." Anna Grace went to tell her aunts that Mary Nell would have to watch the front tomorrow morning because she had to go to the lawyer's office.

The funeral home was empty but for Jolene and Fred. They were talking with Mac Thompson, the funeral home director. Lawyer Gibbons removed his hat and approached the group.

"Mac," Gibbons said as he reached out his hand to Thompson.

"Frank, how you been?" Thompson grasped Gibbons hand and

shook it.

"Doing well, thank you." Gibbons took back his hand and held his hat in front of him. "Mac, I need to have a word with Jolene here, if I'm not interrupting."

"With me?" the large woman exclaimed. She looked at her husband.

"No problem." Thompson turned to retreat to his office. "It's nice to see ya, Frank," he called over his shoulder.

"Jolene," Gibbons started, "I need you to come by my office tomorrow morning for the reading of your aunt's will." Gibbons turned his hat in his hands.

"Will! What will? That ol' woman had no never mind for a will, prob'ly din't even know what one is."

"Well, whatever the case, being Ruby's only surviving kin, I need you to be in my office at ten o'clock for the reading of her will. You, too, Fred." Gibbons turned to leave. "Oh, and I've asked Anna Grace Merriman to join us . . . "

"Who? Who is that?" Jolene called after him.

Gibbons stopped for a moment. "Anna Grace Merriman from over at the River Cafe. As far as I know, she's the only one that ever came close to what you might call knowing your aunt." Gibbons turned from the open-mouthed Jolene and left.

Lawyer Frank Gibbons sat behind his large lawyerly desk, and had been reading and talking about the law and wills and the sort. Jolene and her husband, Fred, occupied the two chairs sitting in front of his desk. Jolene just sat staring at Anna Grace sitting off to the side on the couch against the wall. Anna Grace felt real uncomfortable just being there. She sat and stared at her folded hands in her lap.

"Does anyone have any questions so far?" Gibbons asked as he looked from one to the other of the three in his office. They all shook their heads, no. "Good. Now, I need to explain, and for you to understand, that from this point on, I'll be reading Ruby's words exactly as she dictated them to me." He glanced up and cleared his throat. "That's the way she wanted it."

"Well go on," Jolene commanded, swinging her finger towards the paperwork.

"I, Ruby Wheeler," Gibbons paused to give them time to catch on that these were Ruby's words, "leave all that I have on this earth—"

"Well, gracious me," Jolene interrupted. "She didn't have hardly nothing but that ol' run down cabin. The trailer is ours that we kindly let her live in." Jolene reached out and patted her husband on the arm.

"Including," Lawyer Gibbons emphasized and continued, "all that my daddy give me, which the money is in the bank, cuz daddy put it there for me. I reckon it came from his shine business, but you didn't hear me say that. Anyway, he says you can trust the banks now a days."

Jolene tried to hide her surprise about the money. She cupped her hand over her mouth and whispered over to Fred, "There's money." Fred just held up his hand for her to settle down and be patient.

"And, I didn't spend a red cent of what he left me," Lawyer Gibbons read, "well, except when I had to go down to the doc to see about my infected toe."

"Oh, good grief," Jolene sighed, "can we just get on with it?"

"Anyway, I leave everything that I have on this earth to . . ." Gibbons looked up at Anna Grace and smiled. Anna Grace felt redness rising up in her face, and heard a small yelp escape from Jolene.

"Noooooo," Jolene clasped Fred by the arm for support.

" . . . to the United States of America."

"What!" Jolene shouted and sprang forward in her seat,

"Could you repeat that?" Fred leaned forward as if he were hard of hearing.

"I leave everything that I have on this earth," Gibbons repeated, "to the United States of America." He looked up at Jolene as she sucked in a big bunch of air. He grinned over at Anna Grace and raised his voice slightly. "On account of them bein' mighty good to me over the years, what with sending me a check ever month."

"Well, for lands sake…" Jolene exclaimed.

Lawyer Gibbons looked up at Jolene—looked her directly in the eyes. "And, I quote, still Ruby's words… 'Jolene, you and that good for nothing husband of yours will just have to find another place to live.'"

"Well, I never. Is that thing legal?" Jolene sputtered.

"How much we talking anyway?" Fred asked leaning away from his wife.

"Well, by my calculations," Lawyer Gibbons pushed around some papers, "what with the land and all…"

"What land?" Jolene demanded.

"Comes to just over two hundred and fifty acres. What with the land and all," Gibbons repeated, picking up a piece of paper, "the money in the bank, house, and everything, I'd say Ruby was one of the richest people in these parts." He smiled over at Anna Grace. She smiled back at him, feeling much relieved.

"This is an outrage! Fred, let's go. Right now!" Jolene screeched as she struggled to free herself from the chair. "For heaven's sake," she squealed, twisting and turning in the chair, finally turning it over as she detached herself from its grip. The pair stormed out of the office.

Anna Grace smiled as she and Lawyer Gibbons both stood. "I could just hear Miss Ruby saying all those words. It was just like her. It *was* her."

"Ah, yes, Miss Ruby," Lawyer Gibbons smiled. "Well, now. I bet you are wondering why you are here."

"Yes, it was a little uncomfortable for a while there. But, if Miss Ruby wanted me to be here, then I'm glad to do it." Anna Grace smiled thinking of her friend.

"Miss Ruby left something for you, too, Anna Grace."

"She did?"

"Yes, and I have it right in my closet." Anna Grace gave Gibbons a curious look as he walked across the room. From his closet, he pulled out a fancy, like new, fishing rod and reel. "Ruby said that this was her most prized possession, and she wanted you to have it."

"Miss Ruby." Anna Grace smiled knowing how special it was.

JUST AS I AM

"I'm so mad I could just chew nails." Maggie clinked her spoon against the coffee cup as she stirred. " And the worst of it is," she went on, pointing her spoon at her mother, "there is nothing I can do or say to change his mind. He's just bound and determined to have his way." Maggie blew on her coffee and took a tentative sip.

"Well, sugar, I understand. But, I'm not sure what you can do about it," Betty Rae said with her back to her daughter as she worked at the sink-full of tomatoes she was washing for canning that day. "Margaret, he's your husband," she said, turning towards her daughter, wiping her brow with the back of her hand, "and it's your job to be supportive of his endeavors and decisions." She paused, pointing at her daughter. "And right now he thinks this is the best thing for you two."

"Oh, pooh. What does he know?" Maggie shot back. "How can it be the best thing to take me away from all that I love, my home, my family and friends? It's just frustrating, Mother. What can I do?"

"Honey, John Roy's just thinking about the responsibility of providing for a family now." Betty Rae turned back to the sink. "Now eat up or you'll be late for work."

Most mornings, Maggie stopped by her mother's for breakfast since her husband, John Roy, got up so early for his shift at the flag factory where he worked maintenance on the machinery. He liked stopping by Miss Edna and Miss Sally's cafe to have breakfast with his buddies before work, which worked out just fine as far as Maggie was concerned since she didn't have to be at work until nine. When she got her job at the drug store, her sister said she could use her old Plymouth coupe for a while—her kids wouldn't fit in it anyway. This way, she got to sleep a little later instead of getting up at the crack of dawn to fix John Roy's breakfast and take him to work.

"We both have jobs. We're doing just fine," Maggie said defensively as she moved her eggs around her plate then picked up a piece of bacon.

"Are you planning on renting one of Conroy's run-down houses forever, and what about when your family begins to grow?"

"Mother! We've only been married for two months." She blushed a little as she took another sip of coffee. "And besides, I've fixed the place up real nice for us."

"Yes, I must say, you're a much better housekeeper than your sister ever thought about being."

"Anyway, I'm so sick of hearing all about his cousin." Maggie returned her cup to its saucer with a little more force than necessary. "Ricky says this, and Ricky says that. Come on up here to Detroit where they're handing out money hand over fist. I've got a job for you and a place for you and Maggie to live." She stabbed her fork at her eggs.

"Don't hunch over your food so, Maggie. Sit up." The women let silence grow between them as Maggie sat up and worked on her breakfast, and Betty Rae worked on her tomatoes. Betty Rae slung water off her hands over the sink and turned to her daughter wiping her hands on her apron.

"Do you love him?"

"Of course, I love him, Mother. Always have. That's not the problem." Maggie put some jam on a biscuit and thought for a minute as she took a bite. "Maybe he could go up there and I'll stay here with you and Daddy," she said with her mouth full.

"Oh, honey, you don't want to start off a new marriage that way, with him being so far away." Betty Rae turned back to her tomatoes.

"Well what am I supposed to do? I didn't sign up for this, Mother," Maggie wailed. She wiped her mouth with the back of her hand and stood up. "I won't go. I just won't go."

Betty Rae turned from the sink planting a wet fist on her hip. Maggie avoided her mother's eyes and picked up her pocketbook.

"I've got to get to work."

"I'll see you at the meeting this evening?"

"Yes ma'am, I'll be there. But, I gotta help John Roy run the trotlines tonight. Butch is working second shift. He's gonna help John Roy with the three a.m. run, though." Maggie slung her pocketbook on her arm and carried her cup and plate to the counter. "So, I'll just meet you there."

"John Roy's not going to be at the revival tonight?"

"No ma'am, he'll be laying trot lines." Maggie gave her mother a quick peck on the cheek. "Gotta go, Mama." She left through the back door, letting the screen door slam behind her.

Betty Rae walked over to the screen door, wiping her hands on her apron. "Preacher's got the Morgan Family Gospel Singers lined up for tonight," she called after her daughter.

Sam Tidwell looked up from the pharmacy counter as he heard the voice of his newest employee coming in the door. Doc Tidwell, as he was known by everyone, owned Tidwell's Drug Store on Main Street, and he couldn't believe his luck when in May, just before graduation, he offered Maggie Johnson a job and she agreed. Maggie was a real beauty with her dark hair and blue eyes. She had been voted River Bluff High Homecoming Queen last fall, when his own daughter, Claudia Jean, was the Junior Class attendant. Maggie was personable, outgoing, seemed to know everyone in town, and she was smart to boot. She was perfect to work his cosmetics counter. Right after graduation, Maggie married her high school sweetheart, John Roy Kelley, and came to work at the drug store. Tidwell also thought a lot of John Roy. He watched Maggie come in the front door, on time, and smiled for he knew he was a lucky man to have been able to scoop her up before anyone else, and on top of that she was now a settled married woman. Sales had never been so good.

Maggie walked through the drug store greeting everyone as she went. In the back she hung up her pocketbook and put on her white jacket, which made her feel very professional. She loved her job at the drug store. Besides working the cosmetic counter, she also helped behind the soda fountain when things got busy, dusted shelves, helped in the pharmacy. But her favorite pastime was catching up on the glamorous Hollywood stars in the magazine section.

A new order had just come in. Mr. Tidwell unpacked the boxes for the pharmacy, and Maggie unloaded the crates and boxes for the frontend of the store. She stocked the shelves with all sorts of remedies, treatments, and therapies, but she saved the best boxes for last. When she opened the boxes with little trinkets, cosmetics, and perfumes it felt like Christmas. She kept the makeup counter's glass display case gleaming, constantly wiping off fingerprints, and kept the cosmetics and perfumes in the case organized and beautifully displayed.

J. D. Lowry from over at the grocery store walked in the drug store a little after Maggie finished unloading the new cosmetics. She was studying a new product, "Dr. Bob's Freckle Remover," and wondering if it really worked.

"Hey, gal." J. D. stopped at the counter and pushed his ball cap back a bit. "We sure could have used you last night at the game. It was pure torture without you on the court. "

"Oh, that's sweet, Mr. Lowry." Maggie put the freckle remover on a shelf and straightened some perfume bottles. "Yeah, it was torture for me too; just sitting in the stands not able to do anything. It was really weird being there and not playing."

"Well, we sure lost a star when you graduated, girl. And, I don't see anyone on the horizon that can save us."

"Is there anything I can help you with today, Mr. Lowry?" Maggie flashed a radiant sales smile.

"Thanks, but no, I just need to get a prescription refilled." J. D. looked towards the pharmacy in the back, then turned back to Maggie. "But now you've done gone and got yourself all married."

Maggie knew that the question she hated was following any moment now.

"So, how's married life treating you?"

And there it was.

Now why do people really ask that question, Maggie thought. Do they really want to hear "terrible, dreadful, my crazy husband wants to cart me away, from all that I love, up north to Detroit of all places!"

"Oh, just fine." She plastered a broad smile on her face. Or, are they really asking, "so, how's the sex life?" Surely in the two months since her nuptials, she had assured the population of River Bluff that she was still in the raptures of marital bliss. Maybe she should just answer, when next asked the dreaded question, "The sex is great!" That would sure put an end to it.

"Well, John Roy's one lucky fella. You tell him I said so."

"I will Mr. Lowry. You have a nice day, now." Lowry moved towards the back of the store leaving Maggie filled with thoughts of her marital problems all over again. It was definitely time to get lost in the new *Silver Screen* Magazine.

৪০৫৪

For a week now, Preacher had drawn a crowd each night to hear him speak of damnation and hell fire, sin and redemption, and of the infinitude of Hell. The women came with their slumped backs weary from the day's work of canning the bounties of their gardens, or from weeding and coaxing the last of their garden's compensation for their hard work. They wore flowery cotton dresses with their hair pulled back. Some wore hats. The men, with their sunburned necks and arms, stood about outside the tent until the last minute, smoking cigarettes and talking of hay and corn. Children ran about without regard, tanned from a summer at the swimming hole with their leathery tough soles stuffed into shoes, excited to see friends.

Preacher spoke in the hot summer nights to the crowd that sat eager to hear words that might give meaning to their lives. They had sung together, raising their cacophony of voices high, along with the katydids and crickets, with only the fields and corn to hear. And they had prayed together with loud fervor, asking forgiveness for their sins. During the week, many had come forward to profess their born-again dedication to a religious life. They were anxiously waiting for their baptism in the river at the end of the week.

Maggie pulled her car into the field that had been transformed into a makeshift parking lot. She arrived at the tent meeting as late as she possibly could without making her mother angry. She could only find a place to park out near the road. The nice thing about coming in late was being the first car out when it was time to leave, and not having to do much visiting. But the bad thing was having to traipse through the field in the sweltering heat to get to the second largest revival tent in the nation, as Preacher had proclaimed. She just hoped the chiggers wouldn't attack her on her way.

The music of the Morgan Family Gospel Singers floated out into the field as she approached the tent. Fortunately, she spotted her mother pretty quickly, waving at her from a seat just a few rows from the back. Her mother was beaming with a proud motherly smile; all of her children were now in attendance. Maggie's father, Ned Johnson, was sitting beside her mother, and her brother, his wife, their two children; her older sister, her sister's husband and three young children took up the rest of the row. Maggie was the youngest of three. Thankfully, the last seat on the aisle had been saved for her, providing a clear exit if she felt the need for a quick get away. Her mother gently patted her knee and gave her a warm smile.

The Morgan family gospel singers were singing "Pass Me Not, O Gentle Savior." Many in the crowd were standing and swaying to the hymn.

> *Pass me not, O gentle Savior,*
> *Hear my humble cry;*
> *While on others Thou are calling,*
> *Do not pass me by.*
> > *Savior, Savior*
> > *Hear my humble cry*

As they finished singing, Preacher made his way on stage to stand behind the podium. Everyone sat down.

Preacher took hold of the edges of the podium and surveyed his fold sitting before him. "Friends, brothers and sisters," Preacher spoke up with his smooth north Alabama cadence. He was not a tall man, the podium hitting him just above the navel. But, he was of stocky build with a thick neck. "I have traveled many a mile to be here with you this week. And what a glorious week it has been. We 'preciate all the good singing this week, and all of the hard work you folks have done in keeping the word of God."

"Amens" passed through the crowd.

"Grab on to the hand of Jesus Christ," Preacher bellowed, causing Maggie to jump, "and get the gospel in your life. God is a great healer and he will set you free. Can I get an Amen?" he shouted as he spread his hands wide.

"Amen!" The people hollered back.

"Raise your hands all over this tent and say Jesus." Preacher began to whip up the frenzy and discomposure of the crowd.

"Jesus!" The crowd erupted and many jumped up from their seats.

"Hallelujah!" Someone hollered from the back, and murmurs of "that's right, hallelujah, and Amen" flowed through the crowd. Preacher drew out a handkerchief and mopped his red face. His blond hair was already becoming damp in the evening heat.

"God," Preacher's voice reverberated throughout the tent, "lets only the righteous into the glory of heaven. Only the worthy does he bring home to rest in his glory." Preacher came out from behind the podium and began to pace with great animation. "God loves you, Jesus died for you!" He faced the crowd spreading his arms high and wide. "Amen brothers and sisters."

"Hallelujah, Amen!" People sprang from their seats, holding their hands high.

Preacher returned to the podium and looked down as if in thought or reading his notes. The tent became quiet with hushed expectancy. Finally after holding the silence for some moments, Preacher spoke up. "Last night," he spoke in a serious tone, "I talked to you about the sins of the world that speak to the appetites of men; drunkenness," he shouted, "adultery," he bellowed and brought down a fist against the podium, "and gambling," he spit out in disgust. "And I instructed you men to love your wives and children as Christ loved the church.

"Tonight, our last night together, I want to talk with you about family and forgiveness of sin." Preacher left the podium and spoke of the leper and how Jesus cleansed him. He paraded around the stage reaching such a thundering pitch that his voice cracked ever so often from the strain. He moved with such animation that he looked strange in the blazer that bound him like a straight jacket. Maggie was not hearing his words. She watched as he mopped his reddened face with his handkerchief that he brought from his pocket. He held up his Bible and smacked it a few times. He would open his Bible and read from it as it flopped over his hands. Preacher became more and more animated, exhaling an *ah* after every other word. *And-ah I wish-ah that you-ah wouldn't-ah talk-ah like that-ah,* Maggie thought to herself, grateful that her own pastor was much more reserved. She watched as Preacher pulled off his blazer not missing a beat. He loosened his tie while he spoke of being saved and cleansed by the grace of God. He moved with great agitation as he spoke in his sweat soaked shirt, mopping his glistening forehead with his handkerchief. He stopped long enough to drink from a glass of water that sat on a table next to the podium.

"Now," he swallowed, returning the glass to the table, "we hear gossip about the woman that is seeing a married man, and we talk about the married woman that's having an affair, and we click our tongues and shake our heads at the mention of prostitutes." He sucked in a great breath and bellowed, "all abominable sins of the flesh! But," he lowered his voice, "are these the sins the Apostle Paul chose to talk about in his Letter to the Ephesians?" Preacher wiped his brow again. "No," he thundered. "Paul wrote that wives," he spoke the word in three syllables, and paused for emphasis, "are to submit themselves unto their own husbands as unto the Lord!" Maggie stopped what she was thinking and listened. "Why?" Preacher asked. "Paul explains: 'for the husband is the head of the wife, just as Christ is the head of the church.' Paul goes on to say that wives are to be subject to their husbands in everything." His voice exploded: "Your husband, ladies, is the head of your home, and the wife is to submit and be subservient to him." Preacher faced the crowd and raised his voice to a level not yet reached, "this is central to a God-fearing Christian family! Can I get an amen?"

"Amen!" the crowd yelled, springing from their seats.

"Paul tells us," Preacher lowered his voice to give credence to his words, "that the Lord expects wives to submit to your husbands in everything." Raising his voice again and spreading his arms wide, "you are to support your husband in all his endeavors and decisions." Maggie's mouth fell open and she gave a sideways glance at her mother. Betty Rae was sitting with her hands folded in her lap, looking straight ahead. Maggie's attention fell away for a moment as she thought of her own husband working away at that very moment.

"Now, Bothers and Sisters, listen closely. Everything that you have going on in your life on this very night, Jesus Christ knows about," Preacher continued. Maggie felt like he was in her head and thoughts, or was it God speaking to her? "There is not a man on this earth that can take away your sins. The Bible tells us that if you want to be rid of your sins, you have to come to Jesus Christ! Can I get an Amen?

"Amen! That's right!" the crowd responded. Most were on their feet by now.

"The Bible tells us," Preacher held up his Bible, "that though your sins be as scarlet, they shall be made as white as snow!" Preacher paused as people screamed with enthusiasm. Betty Rae stood up. Maggie was listening and was deep in thought scrunched down in her seat. Her mother pulled on her arm to stand up. She refused, but continued to listen, feeling strange—almost hypnotic— as the words moved into her soul.

"Take ahold of the scarred hand of Jesus Christ and ask for forgiveness. Now listen," Preacher heaved and paused to catch his breath and mop his face. "You may think, that tonight, this very night!" Preacher yelled and pointed to the crowd. Maggie felt that he was pointing directly at her. "You may think that nobody loves you, but Jesus Christ loves you. You may think, this very night," Preacher wagged his finger, "that you are lost and nobody cares. You may be afraid." Preacher straightened up for his finale, heaving and mopping. "But Jesus Christ loves you so much that he died upon the cross at Calvary for your sins." Preacher paused as the crowd swayed and moved.

"Yes, John tells us, let not your hearts be troubled," Preacher continued with a softer voice. "And the book of Isaiah proclaims, and, yes, I'm going to say it again because I want to end with this point: though your sins be scarlet, they shall be white as snow." Preacher signaled the Morgan Family Gospel Singers, "Raise your hands, all that have come to this tent, and give me a halleluiah!" People began moving about, some standing and swaying with their eyes closed, some moving down front to proclaim that they had been born again. Maggie just sat there listening as the Morgan family sang the old familiar hymn, filling the night air with their yearning harmony.

> *Just as I am, without one plea,*
> *But that thy blood was shed for me,*
> *And that thou bidst me come to thee,*
> *O Lamb of God, I come, I come!*

ↄↃ

"Hey, Miss Betty Rae. Where's Maggie?" John Roy spoke as he came in the kitchen screen door. He walked over and leaned against the counter. "She wasn't home, so I came by here and saw the car." John Roy lifted up the dishtowel covering a plate on the counter. He took a piece of cornbread and replaced the cloth.

He was a good-looking boy, standing there leaning against the counter, eating the cornbread. His white tee shirt was smeared with the remains of trotline bait, and his sandy brown hair stuck out in all directions from under his cap. He wore rumpled blue jeans and brown work boots. But even in such disarray, he was quite striking. He and Maggie had been dating since they were sophomores in high school. He played football, and she played basketball. With their arresting good looks, they had been one of the most popular couples in school.

"I haven't seen her since she left the meeting tonight. When I got home I was surprised to see her car in the driveway, but she's not in the house." Betty Rae stood by the sink with a glass of water in her hand. She pulled her housecoat a little closer around her. "Have you had your supper?"

"Yes ma'am. I grabbed something at the house before I headed out to lay the trotlines." John Roy put the last bite of cornbread in his mouth and brushed the crumbs off his hands. He headed over to the refrigerator and found the buttermilk inside. He took a big swig from the bottle.

"John Roy!"

"Oh, sorry, Miss Betty Rae." John Roy sheepishly smiled as he wiped his mouth with the back of his hand.

"I have some pie left if you'd like a piece."

"No ma'am, thank you, though." John Roy leaned against the counter, took off his cap and laid it down. He pushed his thick brown hair off his forehead, and rubbed his face with both hands. "Do you think she's off with somebody?"

"No." Betty Rae poured the remaining water into the sink and sat the glass down on the counter. "She seemed to have something on her mind when she left the meeting. I'd say she's up in the woods. You know how she likes to go there when she's thinking on things."

"Yeah, I do. Where do you think she'd be? We need to get heading on to the river."

"Well, she's probably out by the springhouse. She likes the sound of the trickling water to ease her mind." John Roy straightened up to leave, replacing his cap on his head. Betty Rae continued, "I was fixin' to head up to bed, but I was worried about Maggie. But, now that you're here, I reckon I'll head on up. When ya'll leave would you lock the door behind you?" Betty Rae moved over to turn out the kitchen light.

"Yes ma'am. We will. Good night," John Roy opened the screen door and headed out to the woods behind the house.

The sweet smell of honeysuckle hung in the air, rising from where it grew along the fence line at the back of the yard. John Roy opened the gate and stepped into the woods, closing the gate behind him. "Maggie, Maggie," John Roy called into the woods. "Where are you?"

"Over here."

John Roy followed the sound of her voice coming from the direction of the springhouse. The thick canopy of trees still held the steamy mugginess of the day even at that late hour. John Roy gingerly walked a little further into the woods, waiting for his eyes to adjust to the darkness. Twigs snapped beneath his feet now and then as he moved along the soft, padded woodland path. The effluvious muskiness of the hardwood forest's earthy loam rose around him. He felt a few persimmons squash beneath his feet as he moved along, a whiff of their distinctive scent rose to meet him. John Roy made his way down the path pushing back fern fronds as he came upon the springhouse. Maggie was sitting among some rocks beside the small stream that emerged from the springhouse.

"Hey, Baby. What's going on?" John Roy asked his wife as he bent down to sit beside her.

"Did you know this is my favorite rock in the world?" Maggie inquired.

"Yes, you've told me many times." John Roy bent down to look up at his wife's face, trying to get an indication of what was going on with her.

"Yes, well it is." Maggie rubbed her hands on the moss that covered the rock. "The moss makes it like a padding for a seat. A seat provided by nature." She spread her arms wide. "See how the rock is perfectly shaped for sitting?"

"Yeah, Baby, I do. Maggie…"

"Shhh." Maggie put her hand on his knee. "Just sit with me for a minute and listen. Take it all in." Maggie gazed up through the trees.

"But Maggie, the trotlines."

"Just a few minutes, John Roy. It won't hurt to just sit for a few minutes." Maggie pulled up her knees, folding her arms across her knees, and laid her head down on her arms. "Just listen," she whispered.

John Roy tried to relax and indulge his wife. He wanted to put his arm around her and hold her close. He knew something was on her mind. He sat quietly beside her and listened as she had asked him to do. The running of the water from the spring pushed a fresh coolness up towards them. It felt good in the muggy humidity. A whippoorwill was repeating his song not far from them. Katydids, crickets, and tree frogs chimed in. It occurred to John Roy that he had always taken these sounds for granted, not really stopping to listen. A great horned owl sounded off in the distance. He realized that his eyes had been closed. He opened his eyes and watched his wife, who at that moment looked so beautiful to him, sitting in the dim light. He became aware of, all over again, how much he loved her. Something rustled through the underbrush not far from them. Maggie looked up at him.

"Coon?" John Roy speculated.

"Too small to be deer. They love the persimmon and sumac."

"Yeah," John Roy raised his head to listen. The whippoorwill tuned up again. They listened for a moment. The rustling started again a little closer this time.

"Polecat, maybe?" Maggie whispered.

"Or a bobcat," he smiled down at her. "Let's hope it's a coon." They laughed together quietly and he put his arm around her.

She smiled and leaned into his chest. A few moments later, he tapped her on the cheek. She looked up at him to see that he held a finger to his lips and then pointed down the stream. Maggie turned slowly and could just barely make out a small shape moving towards the water.

"Coon," John Roy whispered into her ear. Maggie nodded. He pulled her in close to him, filling his nose with the familiar sweet fragrance emanating from her hair. "I love you Maggie Kelley." She smiled and lifted her eyes to meet his.

"Well, let's go get us some catfish, John Roy Kelley." She stood and wiped off the back of her skirt she was still wearing from work.

"I'm not taking you out in my boat in that skirt," he teased.

"I'll change while you're getting the boat ready," she took his offered hand as she stepped from the rock. "And, it's *our* boat, by the way."

John Roy backed the boat and trailer into the river at the ferry landing. The ferry wasn't running that late at night, and was tied off on the other side of the river. Maggie and John Roy got out of the truck and went back to the boat.

"Feels like fog tonight." Maggie lifted her nose into the air.

"No fog yet, Mags. We'll be alright." John Roy pushed the small V-hull Jon boat back off the trailer, holding on to the rope attached to the bow clip. "We've been running this river all our lives. We'll be fine," he said as he pulled the boat in to the shore. He handed the rope to Maggie and gave her a quick kiss on the cheek. Maggie held onto the rope and surveyed the river as John

Roy pulled the truck and trailer up into a parking space. John Roy joined Maggie and they climbed into the boat and pushed off.

"Trotline in the usual place?" asked Maggie.

"No, I moved it downriver a little closer to that sandbar that jets out. Brought it off just before Jamison's Bluff." John Roy pulled on the crank and started the motor. "But I have some limb lines I want to check on the way," he yelled above the rumble of the motor. Down river some, he turned off the motor and pulled it up. Using an oar, he began to scull around some overhanging trees as Maggie held the flashlight for him. John Roy checked and rebaited his limb lines, bringing in a few catfish that he threw into a large wooden crate sitting in the center of the boat. The fish flopped around. Water lapped against the tree line that came down to the water. A whippoorwill started his song.

"Maggie, the light?"

"Oh, sorry. Just checking the trees for snakes." She swung the beam of light from the trees back to the line he was working on.

"Okay, that's got it." John Roy paddled out from the shore a little and started the small motor. Maggie faced the bow and stretched out both arms. She felt as though she were giving her river a huge hug. The small motor couldn't push the boat very fast. They were actually just chugging along, but Maggie felt like she was soaring over the river. John Roy smiled and shook his head.

"Maggie, what are you doing?" he yelled. She laughed and spread her arms wider. John Roy couldn't see her face, but he knew there was a big smile on it.

"Just watch for logs and limbs, please," he said, amused that his wife could get such pleasure out of the smallest things.

Further down river, Maggie turned to John Roy and pointed to Jamison's Bluff rising from the water's edge. He nodded and turned off the motor. He brought them in close to the rocks with the oar to a place marked with a red handkerchief. Maggie spotted the trotline running into the water. John Roy maneuvered the boat around and grabbed the trotline.

"You want to get 'em off, or rebait?" he asked his wife.

"I'll just pass you the bait," she answered pulling the bait pail to her side. "I always get stuck by one anytime I try to get 'em off the hook."

"Okay, just have that net close. I feel a big one coming in tonight!" John Roy was using chicken livers for bait along with a few shiner minnows. Maggie stuck her hand into the bait pail with the livers. Slimy, *squoshy*. Catfish flopped in the crate. The stench of river water and catfish filled the air, but Maggie didn't mind. It was a familiar smell. John Roy worked bringing in the fish and rebaiting the hooks with the livers and shiners Maggie passed to him. At one point he threw back a river eel, and at another point he pulled in the big one. He reached down with the net and lifted the catfish into the boat.

"Just look at this baby, Maggie!" John Roy stood and held the fish high. "I smell money," he sang as he danced around with the fish.

"John Roy! Stop rocking the boat!" Maggie held onto both sides.

After a while, they had made their way to the end of the trotline. The crate was nearly full. John Roy pulled up the cinder block that served as an anchor, and stretched the line back out. He dropped the make-shift anchor.

"Well, Maggie," he said as he sat down on the back bench beside the motor, "we had a good haul tonight." He rested his arm on the motor. "I'll get these on ice, and hopefully me and Butch will have the same luck later. We'll have us a nice paycheck tomorrow, Maggie. Maggie? Are you listening?"

Maggie was sitting in the bow facing John Roy. " Look, listen," was all she said.

"What is it Maggie?" John Roy looked around. And he noticed it too.

"Fog's comin' in. Feel it?" She held out her hand.

They watched as the broad river exhaled a dense fog that lay as a coverlet over the river and all that was upon it. Crickets, katydids, and frogs lay quiet. Maggie and John Roy became quiet also. The lapping of the river against the boat was the only sound.

"Okay, let's get going," John Roy said. "Maggie get that flash light and hug the bow watching for anything in front of us. We'll just go slow and easy." John Roy pulled on the motor crank. The motor sputtered a few times, and didn't start.

"What's wrong," Maggie asked. "We out of gas?"

"No, we ain't out of gas," he said, frustrated. "Just hang on." John Roy pulled again, and the motor sputtered to a sluggish start. They moved for a few yards then, the motor died. John Roy yanked on the crank for several minutes to no avail. "Damn it. I'm so tired of working on this piece of crap." He smacked the motor, and then for good measure, he stood and kicked it. "The first thing I'm doing, if we can ever get ahead, is buying a new motor." He plopped down on the bench seat and sunk his forehead into his hand. Maggie stayed quiet. He rubbed his face with both hands. "Okay, I reckon we'll just have to paddle. There's just one oar, so it's going to take a while."

"How do you know which way to go? I don't even know which way the bank is now," she spoke up. "And this light is no good. It just spreads out in the fog. Can't see a thing, except thick pea soup fog."

"Alright," John Roy spoke, "last we knew the bow was heading up river. And we were in the middle of the river. That puts the Toscumby County bank to our right. That would be at the bluff. And that puts the Rogers County bank to our left. So, I'll just paddle up river 'til we get to the ramp." John Roy pulled up the oar.

"That could take hours," she whined. "And, do you think you can paddle in a straight line? We could be paddling around in circles while floating further down river for all we know."

"Well, what would you suggest Maggie?" He was getting huffy about it, and realizing that the fog was getting so thick that he could hardly see his wife sitting in the bow.

"I think we should wait it out. Either here or try to find the bank and tie on there."

"No, we're heading for the boat ramp." John Roy splashed the oar into the water.

"And, what direction would that be in?" she questioned him.

"I'm paddling, Maggie!"

"You're so bullheaded about everything. Like this move up north," she raised her voice. John Roy pulled in the oar and laid it across his legs.

"I knew that was what you were all upset about."

"I'm so tired of hearing Ricky says this, and Ricky says that.

And you… you always think you're right about everything. Have you ever stopped to think about how I feel?"

"Maggie, how can I be wrong about this? What's there to think about?" He waved his arms around in exasperation. "Those people are just swimming in money, dying to hand it over. Ricky says he can get me on at the plant for sure. They even have unions up there, Maggie." He paused for a moment and watched his wife. "Doesn't that make sense, Maggie? Mags?"

"Don't treat me like a child John Roy Kelly. We are the same age, and you can talk to me before you go off and make decisions."

"Listen, Maggie, we'll just go up there for maybe a year. We'll save up a stash of cash, come back here and buy our place. It'll be easy." John Roy held out his hand. "And we already know people up there. Ricky says there's an opening in the building that he lives in."

"Building? You want me to live in a building?" Maggie's voice cracked. She was determined not to cry, but she felt her eyes filling with tears. She wiped her eyes, glad that John Roy couldn't see her that well in the night fog.

"It's an apartment building. He said there's an apartment coming up on the floor above him." She put her head down on her arms. "Maggie, can't you see that this is our chance? If we stay here, we'll be in that dump rental house forever."

"We could live with Mama and Daddy while we save some money."

"No way. That'll never happen. And, even if we did live off your parents while we save up, it would take years to have what we need," he said.

"Well, we could just buy a small house to begin with. We don't have to have a big farm or anything," she suggested.

"No, Maggie. Now this is our chance to make it big. And I have the skills to do the work that makes good money." John Roy stood up and looked over Maggie's head. "What the hell?" Maggie turned her head and saw a broad light spreading out in the fog. "It's a barge. Coming 'round the bend," John Roy yelled. "Maggie, throw me that flashlight." As the barge came around the bend, its bright light swung around and aimed directly at them. The fog spread the light out into a broad expanse. "Hey, Hey!"

John Roy screamed as he jumped up and down waving the flashlight.

"John Roy, you're rocking the boat! They can't hear you anyway." Maggie held on to both sides of the rocking boat.

"Maggie, look for a red or green light. We need to figure out where the barge is in the water. It could be right in front of us. We're in the middle of the river." John Roy remained standing, straining to see through the fog. "There it is! Right there! It's right on us! Red light, port side. It's not going to run over us. Watch your hands! We're going to hit the side of it! Hey!" John Roy went back to screaming, jumping and waving the flashlight. A dark shape rose up like a sea monster from the fog right beside them. With a loud clang the small aluminum Jon boat crashed into the side of the barge. The barge seemed to suck the boat into its side. The small boat scraped along the side of the barge and began to lift and rise up against the looming river creature.

"Hey!" John Roy was frantic.

"John Roy, you're going to turn us over! Stop!" Maggie tried to hang on. "John Roy," she screamed as she saw her husband lose his balance and fall into the water, head first, flashlight and all. Maggie screamed, but the deafening motor of the barge along with the scrapping of the boat against it drowned out her screams. A bright searchlight diffused through the fog from above. Maggie could hear men yelling and gears grinding. "John Roy!" she screamed again. The boat kept rising, its rounded V-hull bottom rolling up against the barge. She was afraid that the boat would turn over, or she would be thrown out. Maggie jumped into the water, grabbing the side of the boat as she went in. She thought that if she held onto the boat, instead of being thrown overboard, she would be able to keep from being pulled under the barge. Lights were on her now from right above. Men were yelling as the barge continued to move past, crashing the boat against its side. Finally, Maggie and the boat were pushed out into the wake of the tugboat that was pushing the barge.

Tears were streaming down her face. "John Roy... John Roy! Where are you?" she screamed, desperate for a reply. She gasped for air, and felt so limp and weak, shaking. "John Roy," she cried weakly. The thick fog surrounded her as she hung on to the side of the boat. She could hear men yelling in the distance and gears grinding. The barge had been grounded on the sandbar in its attempt to miss them. Maggie tried to lift herself back into the boat. She tried to throw her leg over the side. She was so exhausted and trembling from fear that she couldn't lift herself high enough out of the water. The grinding of the gears from the towboat continued. She could still see its lights through the fog. She hung on to the boat for a good while listening to the barge activities and calling for John Roy. After a while the barge must have broken free and it moved on leaving Maggie alone on the river.

She tried several more times to lift herself into the boat. Maggie let her body go limp as she hung on, trying to rest, great convulsions irrupting from her as she succumbed to her tears. She leaned her forehead against her arms. "Oh, Lord," she spoke out loud. "Where is my husband? Is he gone, have I lost him, is he dead?" Maggie wailed. "Please, Lord, bring him back to me," she cried, tears streaming down her face. "I'm sorry, Lord, that I've been a terrible wife. But, Lord, please save us from this!" Maggie held on and let her body go limp again, trying to rest her arms. "Lord, bring John Roy back to me. Please save him!" Maggie cried some more. "Lord, I promise to be the best wife that I can be," she cried against her arms. "Protect him, Lord. Just bring him back to me, and I will be a good wife. I promise! I will go with him up north. I will go wherever he says, just bring him safely back to me." Maggie cried with exhaustion. "I will be a good wife, Lord," she whispered.

At one point in the night Maggie let go of the boat and slipped down into the water. Startled by the water closing in around her, she realized that she had fallen asleep. She frantically pulled herself back to the surface, coughing and groping around for the boat. She was able to grab on again. "John Roy," she whispered, shocked at how weak she was.

After several more failed attempts to lift her weary body into the boat, Maggie lifted herself one more time with all that was left in her exhausted body and was able to get herself high enough to swing her leg over the side and fall in.

She lay in the bottom of the boat, among the dead catfish,

crying—crying out of fatigue, crying for fear of what had become of John Roy, crying from relief that she had been able to get back in the boat.

"Okay," she said out loud after some time. "I have to do something. No more crying, Maggie. Find your husband." She wiped her tears with her aching hands. "Oh, Lord, I think this fog has gotten worse if that's possible." She felt a thump against the boat. Gingerly rising up, she was able to tell that the boat had bumped into the sandbar. Thrilled to get to dry land, she clambered out of the boat and pulled it up on the sandbar some more. Her legs felt weak and wobbly. She tripped in the deep ruts that the grounded barge had carved out. *Maybe John Roy also ended up here,* Maggie thought. She ran around the sandbar, hysterically. "John Roy, John Roy!" she called. She fell to her knees in the sand, and with hands on knees, lowered her head, and cried again.

"Maggie," she heard her name.

"John Roy!" she yelled.

"Maggie!" She could tell that he was some distance away, but the fog could have been distorting his voice.

"John Roy! John Roy! Where are you?"

"At the bluff, Maggie."

"I'm coming, I'm coming!" She pushed off the boat. Groping around the bottom of the boat, she found the oar among the dead catfish. Struggling to get the boat turned up river, she paddled with all her might.

"John Roy, call again, so I can follow your voice," she called out.

"Maggie, over here," he answered.

After what seemed like hours of paddling and calling back and forth, Maggie was able to make out John Roy's figure at the bottom of the bluff. He grabbed hold of the boat and pulled it to the rocks. Maggie scrambled off the boat and among the rocks to her husband.

"Oh, John Roy! John Roy!" she screamed as she frantically climbed the rocks. "You're alive! I was so scared that I had lost you. Oh, John Roy," she cried as she reached him. She held on to him to keep from slipping on the rocks. He wrapped her in his arms, and she cried. Her body racked with great wails of relief.

"I've been calling and calling you all night . . . I thought," she shook her head, unable to speak, lowered her head to his chest again, and cried

"After I fell in, I just kept swimming," he explained as he continued to hold her close. "I had to take off my boots, they were weighing me down. When I got to the cliffs, I must have slipped on the rocks getting out. I hit my head pretty hard, and I think I might have been unconscious for a while. Feel this, Maggie," he took her hand and put it on his forehead. Maggie felt a knot about the size of an egg on his forehead.

"Oh, we need to get you to a doctor. Are you hurt anywhere else?"

"Just some cuts here and there, and I'm sure there'll be some bruises to come." He put his chin on the top of her head and pulled her closer.

Maggie reached up and touched his face. She tilted her head back and looked at him, still in disbelief that he was standing there. "Oh, John Roy, I love you so much! I was so scared."

"I love you too, Mags! You're my girl." He bent down and gently kissed his wife.

Maggie turned and looked out at the river. With his arms still around her, she leaned back into his chest—her home, her safety.

They both stood quietly watching the river.

"It's strange that the river can be so beautiful and peaceful, then it can also be deadly and scary," she pondered. They both thought about that for a moment. "Now what?" she asked.

"Well, I reckon it's more paddling," he said. "You want to check the trotline again?"

"Very funny," she turned and slapped him on the chest. "John Roy?"

"Hmmm"

"I was really scared," she whispered against his chest.

"Me too," he said softly, pulling her in close. "I had no idea what you were doing or going through."

"And I had visions of you drowning under the barge, or being hit by the engine."

"Hey, look," he pointed up river. They could make out a bright yellow fog light coming down river. "Hey, over here," they both yelled at the same time.

"John Roy, that you?" Butch Morrow's voice traveled through the fog.

"Butch, we're here. At the bluff," John Roy yelled.

Butch turned off the motor a few minutes later, and pulled in close to the rocks.

"Man, am I glad to see you," Butch said. "I was worried when I saw your truck and trailer at the ferry landing. With this thick fog and all, I was worried that something might have gone wrong. So, I went up to Maggie's house and got Mr. Ned and his boat."

"You aw'right, Maggie?" Her father's deep voice was like a blanket thrown around her cold and wet shoulders.

"Daddy!" Something caught in Maggie's throat. "Yes, sir. I'm alright," she managed as tears welled up in her eyes again.

"Then you and John Roy get on in your boat and throw me your tow rope. Let's get you home. Your mother's fit to be tied."

ഇരു

Maggie stood looking out the apartment window. Behind her, J. R., her oldest child, nearly four, quietly entertained his sister, Addie, with some blocks on a quilt spread on the floor.

"No, Addie, you knocked it down again. Just watch. I'm gonna build you a house. Don't knock it down this time." J. R. carefully placed a block on top of two others. He was very patient with his younger sister. Beside them the youngest of Maggie's children rocked back and forth on his hands and knees. He would be crawling soon.

Maggie was thinking of what would be going on back home at this time as she often did. There wasn't much to look at from her window. Directly in front of her was a brick wall of the next apartment building. But if she stood at an angle, as she did now, she could look down from the sixth floor and see a tree at the corner of that building, next to the sidewalk. It was early November, and a light snow had begun to fall. Back home, she thought, it would be too early for snow, but she loved this time of the year in the woods. Most of the leaves would have fallen by now. The crunch of the leaves and twigs beneath footsteps would be so loud that she would have to stop walking in order to hear anything. Hunting season would be in full swing. She could still imagine the smell of a fire laid by her father reaching her as she approached the house. She had not been home in nearly five years.

"Mama," J. R. complained, "Neddy just knocked everything down."

"He just wants to join in, J. R. Give him a block to play with. That will keep him occupied." Maggie turned back to the window. She began quietly singing. The children played quietly with an ear to their mother.

> Pass me not, O gentle Savior,
> Hear my humble cry;
> While on others Thou are calling,
> Do not pass me by.
> > Savior, Savior
> > Hear my humble cry . . .

As dusk moved into the darkness of night, she caught a glimpse of herself reflected in the window. She was nothing more than skin and bones from so many years of nursing babies. Her hair had thinned, and was dull, even showing some gray at her young age of twenty-three. Her eyes were sunken with dark bags underneath them. She thought of the night that she was crowned homecoming queen. She was healthy and strong then, and yes, beautiful. That was a lifetime ago. Maggie sighed. She pulled her old flannel housecoat closer to her and retied the sash. She hadn't dressed in days.

John Roy worked many long hours. He was rarely home, and when he was at home, he was usually sleeping. He made a lot of money, but it took a lot to provide for their family. Each check was docked for the rent and payment on the store account, which seemed to bloom out of control from providing food and all of the things that the children needed. The company doctor was also taking payments out of each check, leaving barely enough to live on until the next check. There would never be enough money left for the family to travel home, Maggie thought. Maggie looked at her reflection in the window again. She placed her hand on her stomach. She just didn't have the heart to tell John Roy that another mouth to feed was on its way. She wondered where she would put another child in their small two-bedroom apartment.

She turned and watched her beautiful children. Her heart ached at the thought of raising her children here. The only place for them to play outside was a fenced-in broken-down playground at the back of the building. Its ground was covered in small pebbles—no grass, nothing green anywhere, except for her tree that she watched. J. R. would be ready for school in a couple of years. What would he learn? There was so much that he could learn from his father, but not here.

Maggie used to walk her little family to the Baptist church down the road on Sundays. But she hadn't left the apartment in months now, except when she absolutely had to go to the grocery, or to do laundry downstairs in the basement. Most days were filled with watching her tree, which was now just a bunch of bare limbs with a few dead leaves hanging on, and doing only what was necessary for the children. The small apartment was a mess. Dirty dishes were piled high in the kitchen. She should clean the kitchen. John Roy would be pleased, if he even noticed. But she just didn't have the extra strength right now.

"It's time for baths." She knelt down among her children.

The three children splashed around in the tub as Maggie washed them one at a time.

"J. R.," Maggie asked her son, "do you remember when your grandmamma came to visit this past summer?"

"Grandmamma. Is she coming again?" J. R. asked as Addie splashed Maggie.

"No." Maggie wiped her face with the back of her hand. "But, how would you like to see her real soon?"

"Yes, yes, yes," he responded, splashing the water with each word. Maggie washed Addie, lost in her thoughts. J. R. moved his toy boat around the tub. She took Neddy by the arm and began washing his little arm and shoulder.

"J. R. you be sure to listen to your grandmamma, and mind her."

"Yes, ma'am." J. R. watched his mother. She got quiet again.

"Maggie, you can't take that trillium out of the woods," Maggie whispered. J. R. stopped moving so he could hear his mother. "It'll die." She was looking at the tile behind the tub still washing Neddy. "I know you were right, Daddy. I just loved it so; I had to try. It died."

"Mama? Who's Maggie, mama?" J. R. asked. He watched her wash Neddy's arm over and over. "Mama, you've already washed his arm lots of times."

"You listen to your granddaddy, J. R. He will teach you many things about the woods and the river."

Maggie lifted Neddy from the tub and wrapped him in a towel. She helped the children into their pajamas and dressed the baby for bed. Maggie held Neddy in her arms for a moment, rocking him back and forth as she stood over his crib. She filled her nose with the delicious smell of the freshly bathed baby then laid him in his crib. He was already falling asleep.

"Okay, Addie." The child giggled as Maggie lifted her up and over J. R. who was already in bed. He pulled the covers up to his chin.

"Mama where's Daddy? When's he coming home?" J. R. asked his mother.

"He'll be in soon. He had to work some overtime tonight." Maggie knelt down beside the small bed that the children shared. "Lord thank you for this day," she began the nightly prayers with her arm laid across her children. "Thank you for the health of my children. Lord watch over my children, be with them when I cannot, and walk with them through good times and bad. Amen." Maggie stood and kissed both children on the forehead and turned to leave.

"Mama, wait," J. R. called, "you didn't tell us our story."

Maggie stopped with her back to the children. She reached up and wiped a tear from her cheek, "Oh, J. R., not . . ."

"Please, Mommy. Please."

Maggie turned off the light. She returned to the bedside, moved J. R.'s feet over a little, and sat in the dark, on the end of the bed.

"What story would you like tonight," she quietly asked him.

"Tell us about the woods and river, Mama," J. R. shouted with glee. It was his favorite story, which he requested often.

Maggie talked of the sounds and smells of the woods. She told them, as she had many times before, about the spring, the springhouse, and her favorite rock. She described the whippoorwill and the lightning bugs that they could catch. "The woods will be your friend. They will harbor you and keep you safe. They will provide you with hours of pleasure and freedom. But remember that I told you this," she laid her hand on J. R.'s covered legs, "you must respect the woods, and learn to know them well. They can also be dangerous if you are not careful."

"And the river, Mama?" J. R. asked in a sleepy voice. Addie was already asleep, and Maggie could hear the rhythmic sounds of sleep coming from the crib.

"Yes, the river. The river is both powerful and peaceful at the same time. Learn to read the river. Know what it's up to. You will fish, ride in boats, and swim. You will grow to be strong, and learn to command the woods and the river." Maggie stood, leaned over her son, and brushed the light brown hair back from his forehead.

"I want to see the woods and the river, Mama," J. R. whispered.

"You will very soon, son." Maggie knelt beside him and kissed his cheek. "Very soon. I want you to grow up to be a strong brother, and take good care of your sister and brother." J. R. turned over, and soon Maggie could tell that he was asleep. Maggie stood and bent over him, putting her lips into his hair. "My precious boy," she whispered.

Maggie returned to the window. Her reflection was mesmerizing against the darkness of the night. She looked deep into the eyes of her reflection. There she saw sorrow. An abysmal sorrow ran deep through her sunken blue eyes, veiled by a pleading, beseeching, appeal for relief. She reached out and gently touched the cold window with her fingertips.

"*Just as I am, Lord,*" she whispered, still gently touching the reflection looking back at her.

Maggie slowly walked up four flights of stairs to the tenth floor, pushed open the heavy door and stepped out onto the roof. Snow blanketed the roof, bright against the dark sky. She was drawn by the brightness of the fresh snow. "*Tho your sins be as scarlet, they shall become white as snow,"* she whispered.   Snow falling from the sky embraced her. Maggie walked forward . . .

> *Thou bidst me come to thee,*
> *O Lamb of God, I come, I come!*

. . . leaving behind prints of her bare feet in the bright snow.

HOW DO I LOVE THEE?

It was a strenuous path up the side of the ridge, one that the old man had traveled many times over the last seventy years. He stooped forward leaning heavily on his long, aged hickory walking stick. He made slow, steady progress up the ridge, moving along, in a swaying, bumbling gait, pausing for just moments here and there, listening for Jesse's progress behind him. His unleashed dogs moved around his feet. There were two of them, both Plott Hounds.

Amos Biggers only ran Plotts. He'd been training and hunting Plotts for more than a half a century, ever since he came back from the East Tennessee mountains with his first Plott Hound dog.

He stopped about half way up Dogwood Ridge where the boulders broke the earth's surface. He gingerly sat down on one of the rocks and gazed out across the river, catching his breath. Jesse caught up to him and offered him some water from the canteen.

"Ah, that's good." Amos smacked his lips and returned the canteen. "I think this is my favorite place of all," he said as he wiped his face with a handkerchief. His dogs lay at his feet. "It's peaceful sitting here looking out over the river." His eyes drew in the glorious display spread before him, hungry to take in all that could be seen, preserving it deep in his heart—every shade of green, forest and field, the blue-gray of the river cutting through the

43

green. Each spring the ridge was covered with the white blooms of the indigenous dogwoods. But, it was late summer and green was the dominant color. How much longer, he wondered, would he be able to make this journey? "It's also a good resting place for this old man," Amos laughed.

"You doing okay?" Jesse asked.

"I may be old, but I'm not that old. Just like to take a little breather here and admire the view." Jesse looked at the old man that he admired so. His leathery face was deeply lined from years of exposure to the elements. His gray hair was thick for his age. He was a true woodsman and Jesse was proud to spend time with him.

Jesse sat down near the old man and looked out over the river. His year-old dog, Hazel, sat close beside him. This would be her first run. She had been training hard, and now it was time to see how she would run with the other dogs. She was a Treeing Walker Coonhound. Jesse had wanted to get a Bluetick Coonhound, but Amos told him that he didn't have enough years left on this earth to help train a Bluetick. But now Jesse was happy with the decision. Hazel was smart and eager to learn. They had been up here several times for some training runs. This would be her first time out, and both Hazel and Jesse were excited. Amos was proud of her work also. He was the one that decided she could join in on this hunt.

Amos was a retired timber buyer for several sawmills in the area. He had spent his life in the woods, and knew these woods better than anyone. If he wasn't walking off a timber bid, he was out coon hunting which was his passion. He loved the dogs, the training, and the bond between man and dog. He could tell by the sounds of his dogs exactly what they were tracking—fox, deer, or coon. If they were running cold then hot along a creek, it was probably a mink. He also knew the raccoon well—what it ate at certain times of the year, where it would lay up—and he could do one hell of a coon squaller.

Jesse started work at the sawmill when he was first married, and that's where he first met Amos. They began talking about training dogs, coon hunting, and hit if off real well from the start. Since then Amos had taken Jesse under his wing and become more like a father to Jesse than a friend. He taught Jesse all about coon hunting and training dogs. About a year ago, Amos had heard about a man that had some fine Treeing Walker Coonhounds up north of Farrington, and he and Jesse went up and picked Hazel out of the litter.

Jesse closed his eyes and leaned back on a rock with his arm draped across Hazel. He rubbed her behind the ear. She was a tricolor hound, sleek and powerful. He was proud of her work so far, but nervous about the night's run and how she would perform. Amos said she was ready though.

Amos' son, Charlie Biggers would be showing up tonight with his friend Lyle Beckman. Lyle had a skilled older Black and Tan bitch named Babe. She was a cold-nosed hound that could pick up a trail hours old. She was always a good addition to the hunt, and Jesse was happy that Hazel would be running with her on her first run.

Charlie and Lyle both worked on the barges—working twenty-one days on and fourteen days off. During their off time they worked for J. D. Conroy taking care of his rental property, doing any type of repairs needed. Charlie and Amos didn't get along that well and sometimes things were a little strained when Charlie was around, but Jesse knew that Amos didn't get to see Charlie that often and was always happy to spend time with him, even if it was strained. Charlie was older than Jesse by ten years, and Jesse at thirty-four, was more like a grandson to Amos than a son.

Amos and Jesse made their way up to the clearing where Amos liked to build a fire no matter how hot or cold it was. It could be hotter than Hades and Amos still insisted on a fire. He liked for the men to get together before the hunt and share some time around the fire. They'd talk about all that was going on and Amos liked to tell stories until it was late enough for the raccoons to get moving about. Amos didn't allow any alcohol to be brought in. Alcohol and firearms don't mix he would say.

John Morgan joined Jesse and Amos a little after dusk and helped Jesse gather firewood while Amos got the fire going. John was known as one of the best fishermen around. He was a burley sort of man with red hair. You couldn't ask for a nicer guy—he was always willing to help anyone in need. He didn't have a hunting dog, but he loved being a part of the hunt and spending time with good company, so he joined them as often as his wife would let him.

"John Morgan, I haven't seen hide nor hair of you in a coon's age, son. How ya been doin'?" Charlie Biggers' loud obnoxious voice carried as he and Lyle Beckman made their way into the firelight. Jesse was sure that every coon in the county now knew they were there.

"Aw, fair to middlin' I reckon. How 'bout yourself, Biggers? Lyle." Morgan shook hands around, and traded slaps on the back.

"Daddy, how are ya?" Charlie acknowledged Amos sitting on his stump beside the fire. "Daddy, it's hot as all get out, and here you are with a fire."

"Doin' alright, I reckon." Amos pulled out his pocketknife. "What you been up to lately?" Amos ignored his son's last comment. He cut a plug of tobacco and stuffed it in his cheek.

"Ol' Conroy has been working us like a dog on a couple of his rental houses. But we go back on the barge tomorrow and thought tonight would be a good night for some huntin' before we go back."

"You been off two weeks already?" Amos asked.

"Yeah, but Conroy saw to it that it wasn't much time off. This is the first free time we've had since we've been home," Charlie said as he sat down on the ground and leaned up against a tree. Lyle pulled up a log to sit on. Babe lay down beside him.

"It really is the only free time I've had." Lyle threw a twig in the fire. "We been working all day, and all I hear about ever' evening is that dern preacher. I sure am glad he's gonna to be gone tomorrow. It's caused nothing but trouble around the house with the wife complaining all the time—trying to get me to go every night to that tent meeting." Lyle filled his cheek with tobacco. "I just tell her, 'woman, I've been working hard all day, and I'm damn sure not gonna to spend my nights listenin' to what all I'm a'doin' wrong!'"

"Well, I just go to keep mama happy," Morgan said. The other men laughed.

"Yeah, you got that right," Charlie spoke up. "If mama ain't happy, ain't nobody happy." The men laughed. Charlie poked at the fire.

"She's been harping on me all week, trying to get me to go to that dang tent meeting, so I went a couple a' nights just to keep the peace. It shur's nice to get away from her for a while. And hopefully he'll be packed and on his way by the morning." John Morgan's face shone in the firelight.

A sliver of a new moon was rising through the trees. A great horned owl called from the distance, barely heard over the din of crickets and tree frogs. "Whip-poor-will, whip-poor-will." The whippoorwill's monotonous call echoed through the woods. Lightening bugs flickered in and out of the trees.

"My wife just takes the kids and goes with her mother. She knows I won't be going," Jesse added. "Not after all day in the heat at the sawmill."

"Yeah, I'm aheadin' back on the barge tomorrow," Lyle said, "so hopefully she'll be simmered down 'bout it by the time I get back. It just get's my goat how we're expected to give up our time and attention ever' night of the week just 'cause some preacher has come to town," he added. "I ain't gonna do it."

"Yeah what about that?" Charlie asked as he flicked his cigarette butt into the fire. "According to all of them posters he's got stuck up around town, he's some big time preacher. Preaches in Nashville, Florence, Knoxville—it even listed Birmingham. If he's such a big time preacher why in the hell would he come here to little ol' River Bluff with his 'second largest revival tent in the nation?'" Charlie snorted.

"Yeah, why is that?" Lyle wondered. "Surely he ain't countin' on gettin' much money around here."

"Now I could tell you a thing or two 'bout that ol' preacher if'n I took a mind to," Amos spoke up and spit tobacco juice into the fire.

"What'd you know 'bout that ol' preacher, Amos? You ever met him?" Lyle asked.

"No, sir, I haven't. You know I don't go in for that kind of thing. But that don't stop me from knowing a little 'bout him."

"What do you know, Daddy?" asked Charlie.

"Well, now, it all started up in Beauford County." Amos's strike dog, Moses, stood up, turned in circles and lay back down. He knew when a good story was starting up. "Back when the preacher come to town up from somewhere around the Shoals, only he

47

wasn't preacher back then. His name was Arlie. Arlie somethin' or nother." Amos thought for a moment. "Can't remember his name—won't come to me. Oh, what was his name?" He looked at Jesse for a moment. "Oh, never mind, it'll come to me."

The men settled back for one of Amos' stories. He liked to get together around the fire and meld into the woods, he would say, waiting for just the right time to cut the dogs loose. Raccoons didn't move about much before eleven or twelve. So they sat around the fire with dogs and lights—Amos still used his old lantern—waiting for just the right time to trek through the woods in hot pursuit of a raccoon on the move. This time of the night gave the men time to talk and catch up, and for Amos to tell stories of which he always had one or two at the ready.

"Anyhow, ol' Arlie had him a pocketful of money and bought the ol' Crawford place up near Flat Creek—just north of Farrington in Beauford County. Crawford had done passed on, and his children sold the place to Arlie. Arlie stayed to himself for a piece, fixed up the place, and got the ol' farm agoin' again. . . . "

ℰↃℭℛ

Arlie began showing up in town more often, and attending services at the Riverside First Baptist Church. But most people in the area were still leery of the outsider. Before long he met and married a local girl somewhat younger than himself. She was a quiet, shy girl. Her daddy had four daughters, and Arlie had let it be known that he needed a wife. So, it was said to be a convenience marriage, but still, some thought she deserved better, even though he had a farm and seemed quite capable.

The couple went quietly about their business for several years, always attending church, paying their bills, and not causing trouble for anyone. Arlie worked hard on his farm turning it into a beautiful and productive place. They came to town on Saturdays—she with eggs to sell and occasionally some new chicks, and he bought supplies for the next week. He never ran a bill anywhere in town; he preferred to pay cash. One year, he bought her a new stove. But they never had children, and even though he was still an outsider, people felt badly for them that they weren't able to have children.

One spring around about 1915, a man came to town named Raymond Sinclair. He was with the Highway Department overseeing repairs being done to the bridges and road along the turnpike. The Beauford-Toscomby turnpike had been around since about 1840. The rich plantation owners up in Beauford County got together with owners from the iron furnaces around Toscomby County and built the road from Beauford County through Toscomby County, straight to the ferry landing in River Bluff. They could bring crops, livestock and pig iron to the riverboats on the Tennessee. Seventy-five years later, the road and bridges were in need of repair, so here comes Raymond Sinclair, just as pretty as you please, bigger than life itself.

Sinclair was the project manager for the highway job. He pulled into town in a shiny Model T two-seater and drove right to the hotel. When he stepped out of that Model T, the town's women were all in a dither for he was quite possibly the most handsome man they had ever seen. He had dark hair and moustache. He wore a smart looking jacket, hat, and black western boots. He wore a revolver in a holster at his side. Why, he must be from Texas, or someplace like that, they whispered. He tipped his hat at the women who flushed and blushed as he made his way into the hotel. The women were intrigued—the men thought he spelled trouble.

Sinclair flirted with anything in a skirt—at the post office, at the town diner, in the hotel dining room, on the sidewalk, in the drugstore. The young girls were smitten and loved the hat-tipping, "Ladies" treatment. He took his breakfast each morning at the town diner across from the hotel, and left out for work. He returned from work, changed, and had dinner at the hotel

On the weekends, he spent time sitting out in front of the hotel, watching the town go by, or he walked down to the barber's or the saloon. He was a natural at making acquaintances, but he never seemed taken by any of the young women that followed him around or spoke to him. No, it didn't matter if she could charm the horns off a Billy goat—he just didn't seem interested. It seemed more like a game to him—flirting and teasing the ladies. Some speculated that he might be married.

One Saturday morning, Sinclair was wandering around Main Street seeing what the farmers had brought in for sale. He noticed a young woman standing at the back of a wagon selling eggs and some fine looking tomatoes. He spoke to her. She was shy and reserved. He continued talking to her, and after a while they were both talking and laughing. Some of the women passing by were aghast at the sight of Sinclair flirting with a married woman. But when Arlie came out of the dry goods store, he didn't seem to notice anything. He just loaded up the wagon and got up on the seat without even looking at his wife. She took the cue—said good-bye to Sinclair and joined her husband on the seat up front.

Every Saturday during that summer, they met at her wagon. Sometimes Sinclair was even standing there waiting for them to pull up. Arlie began to notice that his wife's face lit up every time she saw him. When he would return to the wagon with his supplies he was sometimes taken aback to see his wife conversing with a man freely and enjoying it. *She was talking, laughing.* She blushed and turned her head aside in a coy manner. He had never seen his wife behave in that manner. He thought about it for a time and realized what it was that he was looking for to describe it. *She was beautiful.*

On her birthday, which fell on a Saturday, Arlie fumbled around, told her happy birthday, and gave her a kiss on the check. Then they loaded the wagon and went into town. As for Sinclair— for her birthday, Sinclair bought all of her eggs, and took her and his newly purchased eggs to the hotel. He gave the eggs to the cook and bought her a wonderful meal, right in the middle of the day in the hotel dining room.

Sinclair became more brazen with his attentions to the married woman. He was not satisfied with just every Saturday. He showed up outside their church one Sunday morning. Arlie and his wife walked out of the church together and there he was leaning up against that Model T of his. She was stunned to see him. Her face colored with a blush. She looked at Arlie for a moment. Clutches of women were standing about, gawking and whispering behind their Good Shepherd cardboard church fans. Then a radiant smile came across her face, and she quickly walked over to Sinclair. He handed her into the car and off they went for a Sunday ride with the top folded back. Arlie just stood there outside of the church—frozen stock still. *Well I'll bes,* and *bless his hearts* moved through the congregation. Not sure what to do he got into his wagon. As he pulled out for home, he could hear loud talking and laughing erupt from the churchgoers behind him.

Then came one Sunday when Arlie had harnessed the horse to the wagon and pulled around front for his wife. He waited for her to come out of the house, but she never did. He left and headed to church on his own. He sat in their usual pew and took notice of all of the questioning faces that were looking at him. Whispers behind hands and fans traveled throughout the small church. When Arlie returned from church, his wife was not home. She never did come home that night. Early the next morning, Arlie was up at the barn and heard the Model T pulling out. When he returned to the kitchen, his breakfast was on the table—his wife had changed clothes and was heading out for the chicken coop as he came in.

He sat down to eat his breakfast. *Why didn't he just put a stop to this?* he wondered. He seemed mesmerized seeing this woman that he had never known—unable to act. He had given her a good life. She was his wife. She took care of the house and the cooking—saw to the chickens and the garden. He worked the cattle, brought in the hay, and kept the place in repair. They went to church every Sunday. He thought that he had done everything right. But why didn't he want to put a stop to it? Images of her when she was around Sinclair filled his head. She was beautiful.

Friday evening, he had just come in from out back and washed his hands when he saw her sitting on the front porch snapping beans. He walked toward the front of the house. He wanted to go to her, sit beside her, to see if he could conjure up that beautiful smile. Before he could reach the front door, the familiar Model T pulled up. She put down her beans and skipped out to the car. She looked like a schoolgirl. Happiness radiated from her.

After they left, Arlie went out back and saddled up the horse and rode in to town. He walked down the sidewalk and stopped in front of the hotel windows that looked out from the dining room. There he saw his wife with Sinclair.

Arlie stood on the sidewalk watching his wife with Sinclair. The sight of her smiling, laughing, and looking so beautiful again took him by surprise. She had a beautiful smile. Had he noticed that before? She talked with ease, never showing any sign of shyness. And her eyes—they glowed—sparkled even. Sinclair took her hand and held it on the table. Arlie felt a stab in his heart. At that moment he knew that he loved her. He wanted to go to her, hold her, tell her that he loved her. But, he knew that once he did it would all fall away. She would become his wife again.

Two women walked by and when they followed his gaze and saw his wife sitting with Sinclair, they gasped, then giggled, covering their mouths.

"What kind of man would allow such a thing?" one questioned the other.

"I don't understand it. Not much of a man in my book," the other replied.

"Well, he's an outsider. No man around here would allow such a thing," the first one said.

Arlie paced around the house the next morning. His wife didn't come home the night before. *What about breakfast? What about the chickens? It's Saturday—needed to get things ready to go into town—don't know how to make coffee.* He looked out the kitchen window, out to his farm that lay before him, and he cried. His heart ached. He slammed his hands down on the counter. *Why have I not seen this in her? Such beauty! She was here all along,* Arlie thought.

He went out to the barn and saddled the horse. Then he unlocked the feed room, took down the pistol he kept on a shelf, and rode into town. He pulled his horse up where he normally hitched his wagon on Saturdays. The street was busy with shoppers and country people who came into town on Saturdays.

Sinclair and Arlie's wife stepped out from the town diner arm in arm. As they stepped into the road to cross over to the hotel, Arlie stepped out into the road also.

"Sinclair," he yelled. Sinclair turned in his direction.

"Arlie?" his wife said. Arlie put his hand on his pistol that was tucked into his belt. Sinclair instinctively felt for his pistol at his side. He pushed her aside, and she stumbled back onto the sidewalk.

"Arlie, stop this," she appealed.

Both men faced each other in the road. All movement stopped.

Gasps came from people as they began backing onto the wooden sidewalks and ducking into shops. No one could believe that something like this was happening right there before their eyes. Arlie slowly pulled his gun from his belt and held it at his side. Sinclair did the same. All along the street people were peeping out of the windows. Both men pulled their firearms up at the same time—two shots were fired. Sinclair fell to the ground. No one moved for a moment. The whole town fell silent. Arlie walked toward Sinclair with his gun down at his side. Other men slowly began to approach Sinclair lying in the middle of the road. Arlie watched as his wife ran to Sinclair's side. She screamed. She cried. Whispers could be heard . . . he's dead. Is he dead? Arlie couldn't move any further. The sight of his wife mourning the dead man entranced him.

ഇരു

" . . . Well now, a few days later, two men showed up at the hotel, packed up all of Sinclair's things, took his Model T, and left. Ol' Arlie spent the next thirty years in Brushy Mount'n State Pen." Amos stopped talking at the soft, eerie sound of a screech owl close by. The men looked around a bit, then turned back to Amos.

"It was there," Amos continued after a moment, "that he repented his sins and got saved. He began preachin' the gospel to all the inmates. Soon he became known as "Preacher." He held Sunday services for the inmates, counseled the lost souls and gave them hope. He held the hands of the dyin' and prayed over them."

Amos stretched his back, then spit into the fire. "He was released about three or four year' ago for good behavior, and has been travelin' the countryside just a preachin' up a storm ever since." Amos reached down and rubbed Moses behind the ear. "Not long after he went off to prison, ol' preacher's wife sold the farm, packed up and moved away."

"Well, I'll be." Lyle sat up and pitched a twig into the fire. "Who would have thought that the ol' preacher shot a man, just like that, in broad daylight?"

"Yeah, makes you think of him in a different light," Jesse thought out loud.

"I just can't figure how he'd let that happen with his wife and all," Charlie said. "I'd a' had to lay down the law—that's what."

"Well, men," Amos said as he gingerly stood and stretched out his creaking bones. "Let's get Moses here on the trail and find us some ra'coons." Moses stood up, stretched, tail wagging, ready to get to work.

Jesse was in the habit, after a night of hunting, of stopping by his mother's house for some breakfast. Then he would head home after his wife and children had left for church, and get a little shut-eye while they were gone. His wife had come to accept his hunting nights, and his occasional absence from church.

On his drive to his mother's, he thought about the night's hunt. Hazel was a success and he was very proud of her performance. He glanced back at her riding in her box in the back of the truck. His thoughts turned to Arlie and Sinclair as he drove along. He wondered about Raymond Sinclair. He was a brazen, arrogant man, but . . . what? Jesse couldn't decide what he thought of the man—and what about the preacher? Did it take Sinclair for the preacher to discover that he loved her? —to really *see* her? Or, did he just start loving her after he saw her with Sinclair?

Jesse pulled in at his mother's and let Hazel out of her box. She beat him up the back steps and lay down in the shade. He smiled as he looked down at his worn out hunting dog.

"Mama," Jesse called as he pulled open the back screen door leading into the kitchen. He was stopped short in the doorway by the sight of the preacher sitting at his mother's kitchen table holding a coffee cup with a breakfast plate in front of him.

"Mornin', Jesse," his mother spoke from the stove where she was frying some bacon.

"What's going on here, Mother?" Jesse asked. His mother turned and looked at him with an affectionate smile, that beautiful smile so familiar to Jesse. Jesse was speechless. He looked at the preacher sitting quietly at the table.

"Jesse, this is my husband, Arlie." Silence took over the room.

"But, Mama," Jesse stammered, not taking his eyes off of the man. "You've always told me that my daddy was dead."

"He is, son," she said softly. "He is."

54

THE BOGEL BOYS AND THE BIG RATTLER

The low rumble of the beat up old DeSoto could be heard from a good ways off as it came up the road towards the house. Anna Grace recognized it as Joe Dan Bogle's car. Joe Dan and his cousin Larry came by every now and then to see if her aunts needed any work done around the house, which usually meant that they had run out of whiskey money. Anna Grace thought they were the most disgusting, dirty, smelly two people on earth. She felt the deep reverberating rumble of the car. The walls shook and china rattled as it moved around to the back of the house.

"O Lord... those boys are back." Anna Grace heard Aunt Ed's reaction from the kitchen.

The car sputtered and gave out just short of the shady spot under the big maple. Anna Grace threw down her book, pulled back a corner of the starched white curtains, and peeked out her bedroom window.

The boys poured out of the car, stumbling around as if they were trying to figure out where they were and how they got there. Joe Dan was the taller of the two—tall and lanky. If he were a dog you'd think he looked sort of wormy. His long stringy blonde hair looked as though it may have been growing vermin. Fortunately he didn't smile often because the few teeth he did have in his head were a putrid brownish-yellow.

Larry was a skinny little weasel. Sweat had plastered his black greasy hair to his bony little head. Larry walked with a limp from an injury that was the result of one of Joe Dan's drunken ideas of fun—jumping off Wheeler's Ridge to see how far they would roll. Or, it could have been from the time that Joe Dan folded Larry up into one of the neighbor's tractor tires, and with a great push sent him rolling down the hill toward Widow Clayton's house. The tire bounced along, and to Joe Dan's amazement, it stayed upright. Arms and legs were flailing about mixed with high-pitched girl-screams just before the tire slammed into the side of Widow Clayton's house. Widow Clayton was heard to say afterwards that she wasn't sure if it was a tornado, or an earthquake that hit her house. She sure didn't expect it to be a man stuffed in a tractor tire. Either way, Larry now walked with a pronounced limp.

Joe Dan and Larry stumbled toward the back of the car. Joe Dan wiped the sweat from his forehead on the sleeve of his shirt then stumbled back a little quicker than usual looking down at the back tire of his car.

"Well I'll be damned. Look a'here, Larry. We done caught a rattler under the tire."

Anna Grace stretched to get a better look and sure enough there was a snake struggling around from under the tire.

"Let's get it." Joe Dan screeched as he began moving about with great agitation, trying to gather his courage.

"How're we gonna do that?" Larry asked as he looked down at the struggling snake. Joe Dan pulled a bottle from his boot and took a swig then Larry grabbed the bottle, took a swig and returned it to his cousin. Joe Dan slowly wiped his mouth with his sleeve, put the top back on the bottle and returned it to his boot.

"I got it," he announced. "You get in the car. And when I say, you back the car up just a little, and I'll pull the snake out!"

Larry giggled a stupid, excited giggle as if they were really going to pull one over on that snake, and jumped into the driver's seat.

"Now wait until I say. I've gotta get the head just right before you move the car."

"Okay," Larry yelled back, still giggling in his excited alcoholic haze. He managed to mash in the clutch and start the engine.

Joe Dan stumbled around looking for just the right stick.

Finding a nice long limb draped over the fence where it had fallen off one of the peach trees, he returned to the snake. After a few jabs, he pinned the snake's head to the ground. With his other hand he reached down and grabbed the snake behind the head.

"Okay! Back up just a little! Make sure you're in *reverse*, and don't run over my damned hand!"

The car slowly moved backwards, and Joe Dan pulled the snake up, holding it just behind the head.

"I got it, I got it! Damn, would ya look at that!" He tried to whistle, sputtering all over the snake. The snake had his mouth open and was looking Joe Dan in the eye while his long heavy body heaved and curved. Larry cut off the engine and jumped out to see their catch.

"Damn, that one runs 'bout five or six feet!" Larry speculated as he hesitated getting too close to the reptile—moving up and then back.

"Hell, I think he'll run about nine feet!" Joe Dan's chest puffed out as he proudly admired his catch.

"Would ya look at that? I bet he's got more'n five or six rattlers to him." Larry tried to look closer, still keeping a safe distance.

"Are you crazy! They's at least twelve rattlers on him!"

Larry inched up, then back, then up again trying to count the wiggling tail. Joe Dan flipped the snake's tail towards Larry causing him to retreat. Larry stumbled backwards nearly hitting the ground, catching himself on the back bumper.

"Damn it, Joe Dan!"

Joe Dan laughed then suddenly began to move about very excited.

"We can sell him!"

"Yeah, yeah... let's sell it!"

What idiots, Anna Grace thought, just happy that they came across the snake before she did. As they laughed and admired their catch, she could see that the obvious was slowly becoming clear to both of them.

"Now what?" she quietly said to herself with a little giggle. "Takes a while for the brains to get going."

Both boys stood in silence watching their prey. Joe Dan pulled his whiskey bottle from his boot again with his free hand.

"Here, open this," he pushed the bottle toward Larry.

Larry reached for the bottle careful to stay far away from the mouth of the snake. He handed the bottle back to Joe Dan. Joe Dan took a swig and with the same arm wiped his mouth on the back of his arm. Then he held the bottle up and poured some whiskey down the snake's open mouth. Both boys giggled.

"Let's get him drunk," Joe Dan laughed.

"I think you just did. Stop wasting good likker on a damed ol' snake." Joe Dan took another swig and passed the bottle to Larry.

After a few minutes of slinging the rattler around and trying to count rattles, Joe Dan came up with the obvious. "We need to put it in something," he said as he put the whiskey bottle back in his boot.

"Yeah, yeah... like what?"

Aunt Ed came into the bedroom to look out the window with Anna Grace.

"What are those boys up to now?" she asked.

"Watch Aunt Ed, this should be good."

Larry was, by this time, rummaging around in the back seat of the car, and then the trunk, bent over, searching through bits and pieces of auto parts, ragged overalls, empty oil can. Finally he pushed aside a rusty tackle box and straightened up.

"We ain't got a box, Joe Dan," Larry said, "but we got this." He held up a double barrel shotgun. "It's still got that bird shot loaded in it."

"Oh, good Lord," Aunt Ed gasped.

"Well, what in the hell are you gonna to do with that?" Joe Dan scowled.

"Shoot it!"

"Do they buy dead rattlers, ya think?" Joe Dan pondered.

"Yeah, yeah, this'll do it, don't ya know. Just hold it up and I'll shoot it!" Larry was moving into action now as he pointed the shotgun at the dangling snake.

"Now hold on there, Larry," Joe Dan said as he moved back a few steps.

"What? Just hold it out and I'll shoot it!"

Anna Grace was startled by Aunt Ed's voice yelling into the telephone in the front hall.

"Walter," Aunt Ed shouted, "you better come up to the house right quick. Those crazy Bogle boys are out back of the house with a snake and a gun. . . . Yes, a snake and a gun. Hurry!" Aunt Ed returned to the window.

"Oh for heaven's sake," was all she could say as she looked out on the scene unfolding in her back yard.

"Oh, come on Joe Dan . . . just hold it up there."

"Well, aw'right," Joe Dan replied, obviously not able to come up with a better idea. "Now dag gummit, Larry, you watch what yur doin'!"

"Okay, hold it out there. You ready?"

"Aw'right... I wanta get this damned thing out of my hand some how. No wait! Move closer so that shot won't spread out too far and get me."

Larry moved in a little closer pointing the gun at the snake.

"You ready?" he asked.

"Hell no!" Joe Dan looked at the shotgun. "Okay, okay—just do it!" Joe Dan held the snake out as far as his arm would stretch.

"Okay, here we go." Larry pointed the gun at the snake and Joe Dan. The shotgun rang out. Joe Dan began screaming with a high-pitched sound that Anna Grace had never heard before—a real high-pitched ear-piercing squall. Anna Grace stretched for a better view. All she could see was the snake flying and Joe Dan dancing around grabbing his leg.

"Miss Edna, Miss Edna!" Deputy Mankin yelled as he came in the front door.

"In here, Walter," Aunt Ed called out from where she was pacing around in front of the window.

"You two okay?" Mankin asked, trying to catch his breath.

"Yes, but it looks like Larry has just shot Joe Dan." Aunt Ed pointed to the back yard.

"Oh, hell." Mankin shifted his holster off his hip a little and leaned on the window frame trying to get a good look at what was going on. "Well, I'll be. What in the world are those boys up to now?"

Joe Dan was doing a dance limping around the back yard while Larry was running around the yard pointing the shotgun here and then there, yelling, "Where'd he go, where'd he go?"

"The hell with that! Look at what you did to my leg!" Joe Dan was now writhing about on the ground holding his leg. His pants leg was beginning to turn a bright red.

"Well, I reckon I better bring the car around back and carry Joe Dan over to Doc Tidwell," Mankin said. Just as he straightened up and readjusted his holster, another shot rang out from the back yard.

"Got it! I think I got it!" Larry screamed as he edged around the woodpile by the smoke house and started poking the weeds along the fence with the gun barrel.

"Yes, Walter I reckon you should."

‍ℰᴏᴄ₰

The following Thursday, *The Toscomby County News* ran a picture on the front page with an article on page four of the weekly edition: *Bogle Boys Save Elderly Sisters from Big Rattler!* It showed a picture of Joe Dan and Larry holding up their rattlesnake. *"With nine rattles, this is the biggest monster rattler since Ralph Owens came in with a ten-footer from his farm down on Spring Creek. This one came in right at seven feet. Deputy Walter Mankin said the boys were lucky they did not get bit. Toscomby County Agent Robert Weakly reckoned the snake was thirsty and looking for water, given the drought we are having."* There was no mention of the bandage around Joe Dan's leg or the crutch he was leaning on.

THE HANGING

The crack of the rifle shot rang through the air.

"Dang it! Missed again," Snipes Dixon lamented. "Just makes me so dang blasted mad. But, I'm gonna get it." Snipes was always coming up with ways to cuss without cussing. His mama had told him that cussing made a man look stupid, and he certainly did not want to appear stupid.

"Give me that thing," Billy Wayne Callahan ordered as he took the rifle. "Now listen. Wha'cha gotta do," he spoke slowly as he lowered the rifle, "is pull the gun in right up under you cheek. Get your sight right on the target, and keep both eyes wide open—look at that target. Then, and this is the important part, you just squeeeeze the trigger. Don't move anything else. Don't move your hand, your arm, or nothing." Billy Wayne spoke low, caressing the rifle into his shoulder and cheek. He fired off a shot and hit the conciliatory beer bottle on the other side of the creek.

"Hey, now I gotta wade across and set up another bottle," Snipes complained.

"Quit your bellyaching, Snipes," Luke Conroy growled. He was seated on a willow tree root growing out from the steep dirt bank cut into the earth out of the violence of the creek at full run. But it was August now, and the creek was running low leaving behind a wide gravel bar that led down to the shallow run of the creek across its glistening gravel bottom. Luke settled back on the thick root in the shade of the willow, took a sip of his beer, and looked over toward the large log that had been washed up. From there Billy Wayne had been trying to get Snipes to hit a beer bottle for some time now. He watched as Snipes made his way back out of the water, his soggy boots crunching on the gravel. "What an idiot," Luke snarled to himself.

Snipes gained his nickname some years ago when he and his dogs spent two nights trying to catch a snipe. To this day he swears he nearly had several in the bag, but they got away. Snipes and his daddy cut and delivered firewood in an old 1938 Ford pickup. Mostly the boys drove around in Luke's car. But he was very picky about his new '48 Chevy his father had just bought for him—it was black, and Luke thought it gave him a gangster look. But with Snipes hanging around, it was nice to have a pickup truck for them when they needed one, such as today. So Luke put up with Snipes—besides he was just a backwoods half-wit that provided some entertainment value.

"Yeah, I know what I'd like to be squeezing right about now," Joe Sharpe spoke up from where he lounged under an old oak up on top of the bank, "and it ain't no trigger. Claudia Jean Tidwell." He continued whittling on a stick, gazing over in Luke's direction with a mischievous smirk on his face.

"Shut up, Sharpe," Luke barked. "She wouldn't give you the time of day."

"Don't care 'bout the time a day. Just wanna get hold of them jugs of hers."

"Yeah, well Old Man Tidwell wouldn't let you come near her with a ten foot pole."

"Ain't worried about Tidwell neither." Joe pointed his knife in Luke's direction. "You're just steaming 'cause he won't let *you* near her with a ten foot pole." Joe whittled some more. "Hey, Ronnie Lee. Wha'd you think 'bout her? Claudia Jean Tidwell." Joe's younger brother, Ronnie Lee was fishing down near the end of the gravel bar near the canebrake where the creek opened into a deep pool. "Ol' Conroy here's having wet dreams over her." Ronnie Lee kept his back to the others, shot them a bird, and continued fishing.

The Sharpe brothers were pretty rough characters. They both dropped out of school as soon as they turned sixteen, and had both spent some time in juvenile detention. They lived up Sharpe's Holler with a large family—all as wild and unruly as the other. Their sister was a gun-totting, tobacco-chewing, gutter-mouth beauty. She wasn't an all out beauty, but she was a looker. Their father was a moonshiner and the boys ran deliveries for him in their truck.

One night Luke had the Sharpe brothers in his car. They began to talk about how hungry they were, but everything was closed. Joe told Luke to pull around back as they were passing Lowry's Grocery Store.

"Let's go see what's on sale," Joe said as he got out of the car.

Luke knew the Sharpes were just testing him, but that didn't matter. Adrenaline, heart pumping, exhilaration: his first adventure into the life of crime consisted of Bunny Bread, baloney, sardines, crackers, and a half-dozen RC Colas. He never told Billy Wayne.

"I said lay off, Sharpe." Luke stood up and paced around the gravel bar. He bent over and picked up a rock, bounced it a few times on his palm and threw it across the creek in the direction of the beer bottle. He missed.

Luke looked over and caught the eye of his friend, Billy Wayne. He could tell Billy Wayne was still pissed off at him over the Sharpe brothers coming with them. They had words when they met up at Kings Bait Shop when Billy Wayne wanted to know what the hell they were doing here. Luke rode down to the creek with the Sharpe boys, leaving his car at King's, and Billy Wayne rode with Snipes.

Luke and Billy Wayne had been best friends since before elementary school. They grew up exploring the countryside, hunting, fishing, and frog gigging together. They went to the same church and lived near each other. Luke took a swig of beer as he thought about his friend. He was a tall stocky guy tanned from the summer days of helping his daddy get in the hay. They were actually close to the same size, but Luke didn't have the athletic ability or the interest in sports like Billy Wayne. It must be the banker's blood, Luke thought. All Billy Wayne thought about was football, hunting, and fishing. It was his dream to be a UT Vol football player, and scouts had already been nosing around. Yes, Luke thought with disgust, Billy Wayne was free to follow his path, make his own decisions. He was in control of *his* life—he had dreams. And he had no idea just how free he was. Luke hated his own predestined life. He hated the boring, pathetic path that had been plotted out for him from birth—no control, no freedom.

Luke Conroy was the son of J. D. Conroy. The senior Conroy owned most of that part of the county, or so it seemed to others. He inherited the River Bluff Savings and Loan from his father, who had inherited it from his father. The first Conroy opened the Savings and Loan in 1845 when River Bluff was a teaming river port. The bank had survived a few hard times in the past, but though the 1930s were tough on most, it was the bank's golden era. With the current Conroy under the tutelage of *his* father—who was still at the helm—the bank took over many homes and lands as families were forced into foreclosure, allowing the Conroy bank to amass a good chunk of the real estate and most of the wealth in that part of the county.

At times, Luke wore his title as heir apparent proudly, imitating his father's arrogant and condescending ways. But at other times, he would stand in the bank lobby and glare at the portraits of three generations of Conroys and feel a deep rage engulfing him at the expectation that he would follow with his own portrait. He felt rebellion metastasizing deep within his soul.

The father and son argued often. They disagreed about everything. From thinking about his tumultuous relationship with his father, Luke thought about his new car. They even argued about that, but Luke won out and got the 1948 black Chevy that looked just like a gangster car. He was very proud of his gangster car and he knew exactly who he wanted riding beside him— Claudia Jean Tidwell. He thought of her now as he did several times a day. They would be seniors this year, and Luke intended to make her his girl. There was just one problem with this plan. She hated him.

Claudia Jean was the daughter of the town pharmacist, and he was the son of the town banker. It seemed like a natural pairing. But Luke was not interested in their joining the aristocracy of River

Bluff. He envisioned her as Bonnie to his Clyde.

Luke cupped his hand around the flame from his lighter as he lit another cigarette. He blew smoke rings into nowhere. No, Luke had no interest in filling his father's shoes. All he was interested in was the money. It was expected that following graduation, he would begin his internship under his father at the bank. Luke hated his life.

"Hey, I went by and saw ol' man Oliver the other day," Billy Wayne interrupted Luke's thoughts, "down at the garage. Remember his .30 caliber machine gun from World War One?" Billy Wayne asked.

"Hell, Billy Wayne," Luke said, putting a match to his cigarette, "all you talk about is guns these days."

"It's some gun." Billy Wayne eyed his friend. What was it he saw in his friend's eyes? Billy Wayne searched for answers in those fierce blue eyes. He knew they were growing apart. "Browning 1917." He was still watching Luke smoke his cigarette—not listening. "Remember his Japanese sniper rifle. I'd sure like to shoot it—says he ain't shot it in years. But he let me hold it."

Luke took another swig of beer—irritation growing by the minute.

"Yeah well, you should have been with us the other day, Conroy," Snipes spoke up. "We were messing around down on Willow Creek, and Billy Wayne shot a bass right out of a snake's mouth."

"Yeah, okay Snipes," Luke snapped.

"Well, I have to say that one's true," Billy Wayne spoke up. "We were fishing down the creek when I noticed a moccasin near the edge of the water with a bass in his mouth tail first. He was just down creek. I took aim and shot the bass right in the eye. The bass floated away, and the moccasin swam off."

"Well, let's see hot shot." Luke turned and threw his half empty beer bottle high into the air. "Hit that."

Billy Wayne lifted his rifle from where it had been resting on his knees and shot the bottle in mid air with a clean hit. Glass and beer tumbled from the sky raining down onto the gravel bar where Ronnie Lee was fishing.

"Hey! What the hell!" Ronnie Lee yelled. He put down his

fishing rod and brushed glass from his hair as he walked toward the others. He picked up his pace, trudging through the gravel, heading straight for Billy Wayne. He grabbed the rifle from Billy Wayne's hands and turned it on him. Billy Wayne never flinched. He just sat there with solid confidence, looking into Ronnie Lee's contorted angry face—pure meanness emanated from his deep-set eyes. After a moment, Ronnie Lee threw the rifle back at Billy Wayne and returned to his fishing rod. He reached down in his can and got another crawfish to put on his hook.

"You catching us any supper down there Ronnie Lee?" Joe laughed as he called out to his brother.

"Dag nabit, we're outta ammo." Snipes had retrieved the rifle from Billy Wayne and was dry firing the trigger over and over.

"Give me that." Billy Wayne grabbed the rifle. "Stop pulling on that trigger without anything in the chamber."

"We're out of beer, too," Luke said as hurled another rock at the bottle. "Snipes, head on up to King's and get us some more beer. Let's get a fire going before it gets dark."

"Sounds good," Billy Wayne called from the truck where he was putting up his rifle. "I got my gig with me. We might be able to pull up some frogs. Have us some frog legs to put over the fire."

Ronnie Lee had returned to the Sharpe brother's truck and put his rod in the truck. "I'm hungry now. Snipes, have King cut some boloney and cheese. And get some crackers."

"What's the problem Ronnie Lee?" Joe sneered. "No fish for dinner?"

"An' I'll get us some more hollow points while I'm there," Snipes announced.

"No, just beer and food. I ain't paying for you to go up there and buy out the place." Luke flicked his cigarette hitting Snipes in the chest.

"Hey!" Snipes jumped back, losing balance and nearly falling. He rubbed the cigarette out with his boot. Luke reached for his wallet in his back pocket and threw some bills at Snipes. Snipes stooped to pick up the bills from the ground. Joe Sharpe snickered, flicking his cigarette at Snipes as he was stooped over the money. Hit him right in the rear end.

"Come on Snipes. Get in. I'll drive." Billy Wayne gave a hard look at Luke as he opened the driver's side door.

Snipes had gone by and picked up Billy Wayne earlier before they met up with Luke at King's. Luke rode with the Sharpe brothers in their old beat up pickup, and Billy Wayne drove Snipes' truck out to the Conroy land on Okchamali Creek. Luke didn't want to drive his car down the old logging road and across the field necessary to get to the gravel bar. The Conroy land had a good bit of creek frontage on Okchamali Creek as it cut through land that had been in the family since the first Conroy carved his name in an oak tree to claim his Revolutionary War land grant. Okchamali Creek was more like a river in places where it ran broad and deep with bluffs and caves, providing both good fishing and swimming holes. In other places, such as where the boys were now, it ran shallow with wide gravel bars. The gravel bars were a favorite place for the boys to hang out and drink. Many times the field looked like a parking lot as other teens joined in for nighttime parties on the gravel bar.

Billy Wayne and Snipes pulled out headed for Kings Bait Shop up on the highway. King's store was a hangout for old men. They sat out front when it was warm, and they sat inside around the potbellied stove when it was cold. There was usually a poker game going on in the back room most nights complete with beer, moonshine, or bootleg liquor. The boys bought the food inside, and then drove around back to the drive-up window old man King had where they could buy beer.

Luke and the Sharpe brothers began gathering firewood to build the fire on the gravel bar. Mist began rising from the creek as dusk approached bringing in the rich organic smells of the hardwood- forest creek, the wet loam smell of the gravel and creek water. A catbird perched in one of the old oak trees and began its evening call—katydids started their nightly cadence. Luke had just dropped a load of branches and kindling when he heard both Sharpes coming from the other direction.

"Conroy, hey, Conroy," Joe shouted out. "You're not gonna believe what we found." Joe walked up with firewood in his arms looking back at Ronnie Lee who was pulling a young colored boy along with him.

Ronnie Lee walked up in front of Luke with the boy in tow. "Found him in the canebrake, spying on everything that's going on."

"Well, now, what do we have here?" Luke looked the boy up and down. "Where you supposed to be boy? Cuz, I know it's not here. Trespassing on Conroy property. What's your name, boy?"

The boy looked to be about twelve or thirteen. His dark skin glistened in the fading light—eyes wide with fear. Joe had dropped his firewood and was holding the boy on one side as Ronnie Lee held the other. The boy struggled between the Sharpes.

Luke threw a punch that landed in the belly of the boy.

"Speak up boy," Luke demanded. "I said, what's your name?"

The boy fell forward with the Sharpe brothers holding his weight. He became still, looking down at the gravel, shaking, but he still didn't say a word.

"What are we gonna do with him, Conroy?" Ronnie Lee asked.

"He's here on my land, trespassing in the first degree. And being a low down spying peeping tom on top of that. If I were to let you go—hey you listening, boy?" Luke smacked the boy on the top of his head. "All the other darkies would think that it's just fine to trespass over here and peeping tom all you want. No, this calls for a lesson to be sent. Bring him on up to the truck and you hold on to him, Ronnie Lee, while Joe and I discuss this." Conroy was in command. He motioned for Joe to follow him to the front of the truck.

Ronnie Lee watched as Luke and Joe talked. Luke did most of the talking—Joe leaned up against the truck and nodded his head in agreement. Joe stomped a cigarette out on the ground and laughed. Luke eagerly looked back at the boy with a malicious grin on his face. After some discussion, Joe walked to the back of the truck and took hold of the boy and told Ronnie Lee to go talk to Luke. After more discussion, grinning, and evil looks, Luke and Ronnie Lee returned to the back of the truck.

"Okay," Conroy announced as he put his arm up on the side of the truck. He looked up at the sky. Dusk was upon them. It would be dark in a few minutes. "You have been tried and found guilty of trespassing and of being a no good peeping tom."

Ronnie Lee had opened the door of the truck and was bent over, looking for something behind the seat. Conroy looked up at the ancient oak that was overhanging the truck. "Looks like a good one right about just where we need it. Won't even have to move the truck." The truck was backed into the line of old oak trees that divided the field from the creek bank. Remnants of an old fence still showed here and there. Ronnie Lee appeared holding the end of a rope that had been tied into a noose. He tossed it to Conroy. The boy began to squirm around, fighting against Joe's grip.

"Shinny on up that tree and tie her on for us, Ronnie Lee. Joe get him up on that tailgate so we can get this around him." Luke held up the noose.

The boy struggled to pull free, but Joe just laughed and hooted, "Well, lookey here. We done got a tiger by the tail!"

"Hold'um cowboy," Ronnie Lee yelled from up in the tree.

Conroy gave an excited laugh and jumped into the bed of the truck. Joe slammed the boy onto the open tailgate, and together they lifted him up. He was twisting and turning in their grip. Conroy snatched up an old piece of twine from the littered truck bed and threw it to Joe.

"Here. Tie his hands behind him with this twine while I hold him."

The boy's arms were slippery with sweat and hard to hold onto. One clasp of his overalls had come loose, exposing the dark sweaty skin of his chest and shoulders. The boy's struggles began to lessen, but still, there was no sound from his lips except a low, eerie moaning from somewhere deep in his bowels.

Joe had finished tying the boy's hands and placing the noose around his neck when they looked up to see bright truck lights shining from the logging road. The lights turned and began to head across the field. They all watched as the truck moved closer. The truck moved in to park—its headlights lighting up the scene.

Billy Wayne jerked the truck to a stop and jumped out of the cab. "What the hell is going on here?" he demanded, looking from the boy back to Luke. "Conroy, what the hell are you doing?"

Snipes scrambled from the truck. He froze. His hands were full of beer and food. A baloney sandwich hung from his mouth. His boyish, pudgy cheeks flushed and his eyebrows went up. His eyes were wide open as he assessed the scene in front of him. He opened his mouth, dropping his sandwich in the dirt.

"Conroy, what the hell?" Billy Wayne yelled. "You can't do this!"

"I can and I will," Conroy answered with authority. "This is my property, and I can do whatever I want."

"Joe, get him down from there and send him on home," Billy Wayne ordered.

"What's the matter with you, Callahan?" Conroy sneered. "Gotta weak stomach or something? A man's gotta do what a man's gotta do to protect his property."

"Conroy! He's just a boy!" Billy Wayne moved closer to Luke.

"What's going on, Billy Wayne?" Conroy shoved Billy Wayne back with both hands to the chest. "You some kind of nigger lover or something? Maybe we'd better string you up right along with him." Luke laughed looking up at Joe who held on to the boy and laughed with him. "You coming to the little colored boy's defense, Callahan?" Conroy looked up to Joe. "Joe, I think we're gonna need another rope."

Billy Wayne sprang forward catching Conroy around the waist and pushed him into the side of the truck. "Stop this right now, Conroy."

Luke pushed Billy Wayne off and swung a fist that hit him square in the nose. Billy Wayne staggered back, covering his nose with his hands. Blood spurted out from between his fingers.

Luke shook his hand and turned to look up at the boy. "Joe get in the truck and start it up."

"You broke my nose you son of a bitch!" Billy Wayne sputtered. Blood spewed through his fingers.

Luke looked up at the boy as Joe jumped from the tailgate. The boy stood frozen stock-still. His eyes were opened wide, bulging from his head. Tears were streaming down his face. But he still said nothing. "You got any last words, boy?" Luke demanded.

The trembling boy was in shock, no response. He stood stiff, afraid to move, but unable to control the shaking of his body. Tears were flooding down his face. His mouth was open wide with only a silent scream escaping.

"Well, then. You ready up there, Ronnie Lee?"

"Ready when you are. We're tied on tight up here," Ronnie Lee hollered from up in the tree.

"Conroy!" Billy Wayne gurgled, spurting blood.

"Joe when I say go, pull it forward real fast," Luke called over his shoulder, keeping an eye on the boy.

"Let her rip!" Luke yelled. Joe jammed the truck into low and popped the clutch. A scream and great sobs came from Snipes.

The truck sprang forward.

The boy fell off the truck.

And a large bundle of rope fell down on top of him from the tree above.

Joe turned off the ignition. Billy Wayne and Snipes were silent, trying to catch up with what had just happened. Billy Wayne felt tears streaming down his face, burning his nose as they mingled with his blood. He couldn't take his eyes off the boy wriggling around on the ground with his hands tied behind him and a pile of rope on top of him. A great caterwaul rose from the boy, rising into the old oak.

Joe jumped out of the truck and ran to the back joining Luke. They both stood over the boy and let out a loud roaring laugh. Joe reached down and snatched the boy up. Ronnie Lee had come down from the tree and joined in the laugh.

"Lookey here, he's peed on himself." Luke laughed. "Let this be a lesson to you wet pants boy. Mind where you go." Joe cut the twine from the boy's hands with his knife—the boy lifted the noose from his neck, threw it on the ground, and shot off towards the woods.

"Well, now, Snipes what did you bring us to eat?" Luke turned towards Snipes still frozen in front of the truck. "Now, Snipes has done wet his pants, too. We really got you didn't we Snipes? Gotcha, gotcha," Luke leered, pointing from Snipes to Billy Wayne and back.

Billy Wayne had taken off his shirt and was now holding it up to his nose. "Snipes get in the truck," he gave a muffled order. He watched as Snipes got in on the passenger side. Billy Wayne turned and threw his shirt on the hood of the truck.

He struck quick and hard, catching Luke off guard. "You son of a bitch!" Billy Wayne caught Luke around the waist and knocked him to the ground. The two figures wrestled in the lights of the truck. The Sharpe brothers leaned against their truck and watched, spurring them on as if they were at a cockfight. After several minutes of throwing licks and wrestling in the grass, the exhausted fighters separated and lay on their backs next to each other. The Sharpe bothers walked down to the gravel bar to start the fire. The excitement was over.

"What's with you lately, Conroy? What's happened?" Billy Wayne gasped, catching his breath, as he looked into the star-filled sky.

"It was a joke. Gotcha good, didn't I?" Luke laughed. "You should have seen your face. And you and Snipes walked into it all with perfect timing."

"He was just a kid, Conroy," Billy Wayne appealed to the friend that was slipping away from him. "You may have come close to killing him out of pure fright."

"Yeah, well, he won't be slithering around here anymore."

"Is it your dad?" Billy Wayne watched the stars, his breathing becoming more normal. "Or Claudia Jean?" he asked. Luke growled and sat up. "What's gotten into you, Conroy?" Billy Wayne got up, retrieved his shirt from the hood of the truck, and wiped his nose. "We've been friends since we were little," he continued, "and I have no idea why you're hanging around with the likes of those Sharpe brothers," he said holding the shirt up to his nose.

"Just shut the hell up. You don't know what you're talking about." Luke jumped up. "Just leave it alone, Callahan." Luke headed towards the creek. Billy Wayne turned towards the truck.

"Your beer and food are up here," he called out as he got in the truck and drove off.

"You love birds make up?" Joe asked as Luke made his way down to the fire with the beer and food.

"Leave it alone, Joe." Luke stood up after putting down his load of supplies. "He's just being a pantywaist. He'll just piss and moan for a while then get over it. Let's eat."

The boys ate and drank, and threw beer bottles into the fire for a while.

"Did you hear that," Ronnie Lee asked. "Somthin's over in the canebrake." They listened for a bit. Luke stood up and looked in that direction.

"Who's there," he called.

The boy stood up and stepped into the light of the fire.

"Well what do we have here? You come back for more little nigger boy?" Luke turned to the others. "He's still wearing his peed on pants." They laughed. Luke turned back to the boy. He froze as he realized that he was looking at a pistol pointed at him. The boy's hands were shaking—he held the pistol with both hands. Luke held up a hand.

"Now hold..." were Luke Conroy's last words. The boy shot him right between the eyes. Brains spurted out from the back of his head.

The boy turned and ran.

℘℧

Jeb Carothers was eating breakfast with his wife, younger son, and daughter when the knock came at the door. Jeb looked at his wife as he stood—she shook her head. He was surprised, when he opened the door, to find Deputy Walter Mankin standing on the stoop of his small cabin along with several other men. Walter was a big man, standing a good four or five inches above six feet. He was standing with another uniformed officer that Jeb recognized as the sheriff. Jeb looked beyond them and took note of two white men standing just off the porch.

"Jeb, this here is Sheriff McCord," Mankin said as he indicated the man standing next to him. Jeb noticed two more white men standing off to the side a little. "The Sheriff has come down here from Farrington to help us out." Mankin removed his hat and wiped his forehead with his sleeve. "There was an incident last night," he continued, "and we're going 'round to all of the colored families talking to boys between the ages of ten and fifteen. Is this your son here?" he said pointing to Jeb's son standing at his side. "He looks pretty young. How old is he?"

"Nine," Jeb answered, putting his arm around his son—pulling

73

him close. He glanced back at his wife standing at the table with their daughter. "What sort of incident?" he asked Mankin.

"Don't you have another son, Jeb?" Mankin asked.

"Yessuh, but he ain't here right now." Jeb could feel sweat running down his back. His pulse quickened.

"When was the last time you saw him?"

"He came through here yesterd'y evening, a little after dark it was. We was sitting on the porch, me and my wife, the young'uns were catching lightnin' bugs. We hear'd him come in through the back. Then he left again. He hasn't come back in yet," Jeb said. "I'm sure he's off fishing. It ain't unus'l for him to be out at night fishing or such. He be in here pretty soon lookin' for a big breakfast," Jeb added hastily. He realized that he was talking too much out of his nervousness. He pulled his son closer.

Mankin looked over at the sheriff.

"Jeb, do you own a gun?" Sheriff McCord asked.

Jeb hesitated and looked down at his son. His boy looked up at him. "Yessuh, I do," he said reluctantly.

"Hey, now! What's this nigger doing with a gun?" one of the other two men asked as he moved forward.

"Now, Lyle, just back up. We'll handle this." Mankin held his hand out to back the man up. Lyle Becker and Charlie Biggers worked for J. D. Conroy, and had been accompanying the Sherriff and Deputy throughout the morning. Jeb noticed there was also a group of white men standing around several trucks parked up on the road.

"I was a member of the 452nd Artillery Battalion during the war. It's my service pistol," Jeb explained.

"When was the last time the gun was fired?" Mankin asked.

"I shot it a week or so ago. Killed a rattler out back."

"Have you taught your boys how to fire the gun?"

"No, they've never fired it." Jeb tried to appear calm, but his insides were churning. This situation did not bode well. He signaled for his boy to go to his mother at the back of the room. The young boy ran over to his mother.

"I'll need to see it," McCord said as he stepped forward to enter the home. Jeb lingered for a moment and then moved away to make room for the deputy and sheriff to enter his home. Mankin told the other men to stay off in the yard.

"I keep it in a box in the other room." Jeb nervously pointed the men to the only other room in the small house. They followed him into the tiny room. "It stays under my bed," Jeb said as he reached for the box. He pulled an old beat-up tin box, laid it on the bed and opened it. It was empty.

"Daddy," his young daughter called for him. "Daddy."

Jeb was stunned at the sight of the empty box.

"What sort of incident happened last night?" Jeb's voice shuddered.

"J. D. Conroy's boy, Luke, was shot and killed by a young colored boy down on Okchamali Creek." Mankin picked up the box. "Jeb, I need to see your boy now."

"Daddy, Daddy," his daughter called again as the men walked back into the other room. Mankin carried the empty box. Jeb signaled for his wife to quiet the girl.

"He's not here," Jeb repeated, watching his wife. "But, he's a good boy. He wouldn't, couldn't, do such..."

"Daddy!" his young daughter interrupted from where she was standing in the doorway that led to the screened in back porch where the children slept in the summer. Jeb held up his hand to his daughter as he watched the sheriff. "But, Daddy, that's what I'm trying to tell you. He's done run away!"

"What?" several of them said at the same time.

"All of his things are gone, even his snakeskin that stays by his bed. His clothes and everything, gone," she squealed. "He's done run away!"

That night, Jeb cradled his wife close to him as they lay in bed. He listened to her soft crying. Her tears echoed the pain he felt in his heart. He just could not put together any reason that would call for his son to murder a white boy.

"He's out there alone and afraid," she spoke softly through her tears. "They're hunting him down like an animal." Her body shook with pain and fear for her son. "It couldn't have been him. I just refuse to believe it." She pulled in a deep breath. "Why didn't he talk to us? Why would he just leave?"

"I suppose he wanted to take the danger away from us," he

answered his wife.

"But why would he do such a thing?" she verbalized the question that had plagued him all night.

"I don't know. He's a good boy. Only God knows."

There was a loud crash—the sound of glass breaking. Jeb jumped from his bed. Another crash of glass breaking came from the other room. Jeb saw flames erupting through the room. His wife screamed. His two children ran in from the porch, eyes large with fear. Jeb grabbed up his daughter, looking around. The flames clutched at the surroundings, pulling all in its path into its greedy grip.

Out the back, Jeb thought, just as a loud explosion of fire began to engulf the tiny back porch. He started for the bedroom in order to go out the side window. He pulled his son close. Where was his wife? Another crash of glass came from his bedroom. His daughter screamed and clawed at this neck. He turned to find his wife coming out of the bedroom with her mother's quilt. They were caged in with the only exit—the front door.

"We've gotta get out," his son yelled as he ran to the door.

"No!" Jeb yelled after him. The boy flung open the door and ran out as Jeb and his wife made their way to the door.

Two rifle shots splintered through the night air. His wife screamed and ran out the door. Jeb tried to yell—his voice froze. *Wife get down, running for door, sweat in eyes, can't see, daughter clawing, screaming, breathing hard, my family, bright lights, son hide!* Lights from several cars and trucks blinded him as he stood on the porch. The vehicles began to pull away—men laughing, screaming, shouting obscenities into the night. He held his daughter close. After the vehicles made their way further down the road, the only sounds left were the crackling of the fire that was gorging itself on his home and meager possessions. Then a mother's long mournful wail rose into the night sky. In the glow of the fire, he caught sight of her crouched beneath the sycamore tree. She was clutching their son to her bosom, rocking him as she wailed. "Oh, Lord. Oh Lord," she cried. Jeb watched her stroke his small head as he felt the life being sucked out of him—collapsed to his knees—his daughter clung to him—great convulsions erupting from him as he dissolved into tears.

His son was dead.

෩ଓ

Jeb Carothers walked through the door of the Sheriff's Office. He removed his hat and reached into the bib pocket of his overalls pulling out a well-worn, folded paper. "Dep'ty Mankin, I come by today to tell you we had a letter from my boy." Jeb held the paper in his hands with his hat, not looking directly at Mankin. "He say he was sorry for the heartbreak he brought on his mother. He also say he hopped a barge and then hopped other barges to the Mississippi, and went as far north as the river would take him."

Walter Mankin leaned back in his chair. The chair creaked under his weight. He took a long draw on his cigarette and exhaled a long stream of smoke from his mouth and nose. A permanent brown haze hung in the air. He watched Jeb standing before him, head lowered, no eye contact. Crevices of pain could be traced on the father's face. Mankin leaned forward and put out his cigarette in an overflowing ashtray.

"He's probably in New Orleans, or St. Louis."

"He say he has a job," Jeb went on, as he returned the letter to his pocket, "and that he took my gun with him." Silence hung in the air. Thick silence. "He's young but he strong. I 'spect he'll be able to take care of hisself."

"Yes, I'd say you're right about that." Mankin scratched his head and leaned back in his chair crossing his legs. A ponderous pause ensued. Mankin knew what Jeb wanted to ask.

"Is there any news on them men that kil't my boy and burned my house down?" Jeb asked Mankin the question that he had asked many times over the past five or six weeks.

"No, the whole town has clammed up. They're not gonna give up those that done it. I think it's seen as a case of an eye for an eye."

"Yessuh," he murmured quietly. "But I have lost both my boys, my house, and everything I own." He fumbled with his hat he held in front of him.

"Jeb, I ain't looking for your boy, and there's not going to be any resolution to what happened to your family."

Jeb stood quiet and thought for a moment. A grimace of pain spread across his face. He cleared his throat. "We been staying with my wife's family. It's a little tight, but we make do. I can't find work now." He stood quiet again. "The other day a car full of boys threw bottles at my daughter as she was walking home from the store." He looked down at the floor. "So, I wanted to let you know that we are leaving town. I reckon we'll head up to Nashville, and see if we can find work." He made a slight move toward the door.

"Jeb," Mankin's voice stopped him. "I talked with those boys that were there when your boy shot Conroy. I pushed 'em pretty hard. They told me what happened that night. Billy Wayne Callahan and Snipes Dixon confirmed what they said. I haven't told anyone else. Don't really see any need in it. And I don't reckon those boys will do much talking about it. But, I want you to know." Mankin then proceeded to tell Jeb about the hanging. The man stood, held his hat with his hands folded in front of him, listening with his head slightly bowed. Tears filled his eyes threatening to spill over as he listened. And when Mankin finished the man stood still for a moment, tears flowing unheeded.

"I knowd he was a good boy," he said quietly. "I knowd there must'a been somethin' happen to make him do such a thing. Thank you kindly for tellin' me." He stood there for a moment, his head drooped, and taking a handkerchief from his back pocket, wiped his face.

Something made Mankin stand and lean toward the grieving man in front of him. He paused. Then he came from behind his desk and placed his hands on his hips as he watched the man. After a moment, Mankin extended his hand to Jeb. Jeb hesitated, then clasped the deputy's hand and—raising his head—their eyes met. Nothing more was said between the men. Jeb turned and walked out the door.

JAMISON'S BLUFF

Esther could see through the screen door, as she walked down the hall, a man standing on the front porch. He was a large man with a round middle. His face was bright red with small beady eyes. He wore a white linen suit, complete with white hat and shiny white shoes.

"Oh, Lord, what he trying to sell?" she said to herself, wiping her hands on a kitchen towel, then smoothing her white uniform.

"Good afternoon," he spoke before she could say no thank you. "I'm here to see Miss Evelyn Jamison."

"We ain't in'erested in buyin' nothing," Esther spoke through the screen door.

"Now see here, Missy." He removed his hat and pointed it at her. "I ain't here to sell anything." He pulled out a handkerchief and wiped his glistening forehead and his partially balding head. "Now you go and tell your employer that she has a visitor, and that it's imperative that she see me."

"Miss Evelyn ain't taking no visitors today, but if'n you leave your name, I'll be sure to tell her you stopped by." Esther moved to close the front door. The red-faced man yanked open the screen door and jammed the closing door with a shiny white shoe.

"Well, I never," Esther gasped. "What do you . . . "

"Now you go on," he demanded. "Ya hear. Go tell her she has

a visitor," he spoke as he stepped into the doorway. Esther eyed the man closely, twisting the towel in her hands, trying not to give up any more ground as he stepped on into the foyer. "Go on, now," he repeated, shooing her on.

"You just stay right cher, you hear." Esther pursed her lips, placed one hand on her hip, flapping the towel at him with the other.

"Don't give me no sass, girlie. Just go tell her I'm here."

Esther turned and headed down the hallway, mumbling to herself, turning every few steps to make sure the visitor was staying put. She pushed open the screen door at the back of the house opposite the front door where she found Miss Evelyn sitting out on the back veranda over looking the Tennessee River.

"Miss Evelyn," Esther said.

Evelyn continued her thoughts—the ill repair of the house. Her gaze fell upon the large backyard. The veranda needed painting, a few columns were loose, and at the end of the yard were the remnants of a few fence posts covered with honeysuckle. She needed to get Clovis to clean those out—no need for a fence any longer. Evelyn thought of playing there as a girl with her brother and cousins.

The house was built on a large bluff that loomed over the Tennessee River below, and the fence was built to contain young children so that they might not get to running around and run right off the bluff, dropping down to the rocks below. She still lived in the same house, more of a mansion, that she was born in, known simply as the "Jamison Place."

The family had built a fortune through a successful barging company, and before that, riverboats. At one time the family was very wealthy, but all of that was before her brother became the age that he could spend it.

"Miss Evelyn?"

"Yes?" Evelyn brought herself back to the present.

"You have a visitor, Miss Evelyn," Esther said.

"Well for heaven's sake, who in the world—?"

"He won't say his name. Just barged right in! Says it's 'perative that you see him."

"Goodness me!" Evelyn said as she patted her hair. "Well,

alright, show him into the parlor."

Evelyn stood in the parlor doorway a few minutes later, watching the large man standing at the fireplace with his back to her. She didn't recognize him. She watched him for a moment as he was looking rather closely at the ornate Ansonia mantle clock, touching all the details. He pulled out his pocket watch and compared the time.

"Well, now," Evelyn said causing the man to turn to her. "To what do I owe this pleasure Mr. . . . . ?"

"Charlie Monroe," he said as he returned the watch to its pocket.

"Mr. Monroe, a pleasure to meet you. Won't you sit down?" Evelyn indicated the red Duncan Phyfe sofa as she moved to have a seat on one of the pair of Victorian chairs across from the sofa. She chose the one nearest the fireplace. Evelyn watched the large man sit back on the sofa, worried that it might not support him. The elegant sofa creaked as he sprawled back into the plush cushions, spreading his arm across the back, then propped his ankle on the knee of the other leg. Evelyn was offended by his familiar behavior in her home. Evelyn traded glances with Esther, standing at the door, who looked thoroughly disgusted.

"Would you like some sherry, Mr. Monroe?"

"Sherry?" he snorted. "No, something cold to drink. Maybe some iced tea?"

"Esther, sherry for me and iced tea for Mr. Monroe." Evelyn looked at Esther with her best hostess smile. Esther grumbled something and left the room. "So, Mr. Monroe, what brings you to River Bluff, and specifically to see me?"

"I've been in town a few days now," Monroe indifferently replied as he surveyed the room, not looking directly at his hostess.

"I see." Evelyn began to feel very uncomfortable in the man's presence. She watched him, as he remained aloof, leaning back into the sofa, perusing the room from one end to the other. Her mind was racing, trying to account for his behavior. She was definitely not the center of his attention. Yes, his behavior implied an *arrière-pensée*. She smiled thinking that Madame Bataille would be proud of her vocabulary. But back to matters at hand—was he casing the place? Preparing to come back with his gang and rob her blind? Deputy Mankin had told Evelyn that he was concerned about her living in that big mansion by herself after her father passed away just a couple of months ago. But what could she do? It was her home, and here she would stay. Just as she was wondering if she should slip away for a moment on some pretense and call the deputy, Esther came into the parlor with a silver service, which she placed on the table in front of the sofa. Of course she would bring in the best silver and china when there was a thief among us, Evelyn thought.

"Thank you, Esther." Well there was nothing for it, but to be the polite hostess while this man was making a mental list of the things that he would take. "Your tea, Mr. Monroe," Evelyn said as she passed him his glass of tea. Monroe dropped his foot from his knee and sat forward with such a thunder that she thought the Gone With the Wind lamp on the side table might be knocked over. Esther crinkled up her nose at the man as she handed Evelyn her sherry in one of her finest cut crystal wine glasses. Monroe had already gulped down half of his tea and was devouring Esther's lovely cucumber sandwiches, cut to small finger-sandwich size, served on Evelyn's mother's dainty silver serving platter. He was eating three small sandwiches at a time, eyeing the silver and crystal as he ate.

"You've just been in town a few days," Evelyn continued after Esther had left. "Where are you from, Mr. Monroe?"

"Came in from Memphis," Monroe said with his mouth full of two more sandwiches.

"Memphis. I have a brother in Memphis. He's a cotton broker. Maybe you know him, Joe Jamison?" Evelyn watched Monroe finish the rest of his tea, run his tongue around his teeth, along with a few smacking noises, and resume his sprawled-out lounging posture on the sofa. "Oh, goodness!" Evelyn placed her sherry glass on the silver tray. "You haven't come with news of my brother have you. Has any harm come to him?"

"Oh, I'm sure he's doing just fine. Just where he's doing it is the question," Monroe said, still not looking directly at Evelyn. She couldn't detect if it was rudeness or arrogance at the root of this appalling behavior. She did not like this man one bit—him or his boorish behavior. After saying something like that about her brother he just sat there, looking around. Well she was not going to play into this behavior by begging him to talk to her. He came to see her after all. Evelyn took another sip of sherry and looked out the side window. After some time of this war of wills, he finally sat up with exaggerated frustration.

"Now see here, Miss Jamison," he started off which just put a rod down her back. She sat stiffly with her hands in her lap trying to endure this impolite, rude man as any good southern hostess is given to do.

"Your brother," he continued, "did set up his cotton brokerage business. He rented a warehouse, set up an office, and did very well for himself. Business has been good these years after the war. And with 1950 just around the corner, I think businesses will be walking in tall cotton, if you get my meaning." Monroe chuckled at his own humor, snatched up the last two cucumber sandwiches, popped them in his mouth, and continued speaking and chewing at the same time. "Your brother came to me to invest in his business while he was getting things off the ground. I knew him as a regular at my back room. I own a nightclub in Memphis, and I have a special back room especially for men to play cards. Anyway, I decided to invest in the business and lent him the initial amount to get him going. It seemed like a good investment. He told me all about your family business, and he seemed to know what he was doing, or so I thought."

Well, here we go. Joe had gotten himself in trouble again. Evelyn closed her eyes mentally preparing herself for the blow. Joe was the older sibling, and had single-handedly undone generations of family business.

Evelyn's great-great-grandfather landed on the bluffs of the Tennessee River just below where the mansion now stood in 1809. Captain Benjamin Jamison started his shipping business from a cove right down from the bluffs. He made many profitable trips up the Tennessee to the Ohio, down the Mississippi to Memphis, or down the Cumberland to Nashville. He once made the trip all the way to New Orleans. However, at that time the only option was to sell the ship, buy horses, and make the hard and dangerous trip back on the Natchez Trace. The perils of travel on the Trace at that time were great. Men leaving New Orleans with a big profit in their saddlebags were easy targets for bandits. One trip was enough for Jamison. Later when steamboats made up-river travel possible, and after the Livingston-Fulton Monopoly was disbanded, Jamison invested in steamboats. He could make the trip to New Orleans in eighteen days, and the return trip in twenty-two. The Jamison Shipping Company was born.

In later years a fleet of barges was added and an office was set up in New Orleans. Through the years, each generation added to the company, which did very well for the family. Evelyn's great-grandfather built the mansion up on the bluff looking down over the river. And Evelyn's grandfather and her father bought property down river that included the cove with the intention of starting a company for building and repairing barges. But, Jamison Barge Company never got off the ground. That was about the time that Joe began the systematic ruination of the family business and fortune.

Joe was sent to Tulane in New Orleans to study and train in the shipping business at the family's New Orleans office. He soon married his college sweetheart who came from a very prominent New Orleans family, and she loved spending money, entertaining, and keeping up appearances. The newlyweds built a monstrous, lavish place in New Orleans, importing fine expensive furnishings. Joe sapped the business of its money, finally leading it into bankruptcy and him into divorce. The only thing the family had left was the mansion in River Bluff and the property intended for the barge company that was never conveyed to Jamison Shipping.

"And why does any of this bring you to see me, Mr. Monroe?" Evelyn asked as she opened her eyes, trying to see the connection.

"I went by to see your brother a couple of weeks ago since he was coming up on sixty days behind on his payments."

Evelyn still sat rigidly in her chair trying not to fidget. Fear was building just as surely as she knew that anything of a negative type having to do with her brother would surely affect her in a negative way. Evelyn had been sent, at the age of fifteen, to the prestigious Ward-Belmont School for Women, a renowned ladies' finishing school in Nashville, attracting young ladies from aristocratic families across the south. She studied French with a passion with her beloved French tutor, Madame Bataille. She and Madame planned on touring Europe after Evelyn's coming-out ball and graduation. Evelyn's plans never materialized because, unknown to her, Joe Jamison at that very same time was busy destroying her future down in New Orleans. She was called home—the trip was off, and her time as a Southern debutante was not to be. Was there more loss that he could bring upon her? He had taken her future— her life. Evelyn tried to concentrate on what Monroe was saying. Her hands shook in her lap.

"So, there you have it. All that was left was a door to an empty office that said 'Joseph P. Jamison, Cotton Broker'. I've tried everything I know to find him. All I could find out is that he had flown the coop and is out in Arizona somewhere," Monroe continued.

"Well, I'm sorry that you have come all this way for nothing, but my brother is not here—has not been here for years. I never could get hold of him when our father died a couple of months ago. So, he didn't even come home for our father's funeral." Evelyn made a move to rise from her chair. "As you see, Mr. Monroe, I can be of no help to you. I don't have any idea where my brother is."

Monroe didn't make any move to leave. Indeed, he sat back into the sofa causing it to creak again under the strain of his weight. He picked up his tea glass and shook it! Evelyn let out a long breath and rang the small dainty bell on her side table. After Esther left the room having delivered Monroe another glass of tea, which he didn't bother to say thank-you for, Monroe reached into his jacket pocket and produced some papers.

"I'm not in the practice of just lending money, Miss Jamison, without some sort of collateral." Monroe flipped through the pages. "This is your brother's loan paperwork in which he secured his loan with an expectation of inheritance." Monroe sat back again, letting Evelyn digest what he had just said.

"Expectation of what inheritance, Mr. Monroe?" Evelyn stammered. "He has taken *everything* from this family. There is nothing to expect."

"Well, and may I say that I'm real sorry to hear of your father's death, but your brother's inheritance would include this home, the land that it's on, everything in the home, and the forty-five acres down river."

Evelyn felt the life being sucked out of her. Indeed there was more that her brother could take! She felt faint.

"So, Mr. Monroe, it appears that you have come to take my home from me to satisfy my brother's debt," Evelyn said when she was finally able to speak.

"Well not all of it, just half of all of it—your brother's inheritance."

"And what do you propose we do? Cut the house in half?" Evelyn was trying to hold back tears that were threatening to fall. She vowed that she would never let this man see her tears, though.

"No." Monroe gave a deep belly laugh. "We could just come to terms as to the value of everything and you can just pay me my half."

"Mr. Monroe, my brother, through the years, has drained this family of all resources what with his divorce and the bankruptcy of the business. I'm sorry to say that I don't have that amount of cash on hand." Again Evelyn made a move to get up as to encourage the man to leave. "So, again I say I'm sorry but it seems that you have wasted a trip. You can see that I am unable to help you. Now I really must retire. This has been a most stressful meeting." Evelyn stood. "I will have Esther show you out."

"Now wait just a minute. We have more to discuss." Monroe sat forward on the sofa.

"What in heaven's name could be left, Mr. Monroe?"

"We have not discussed the sale of the house and land," Monroe rooted around on the platter picking up crumbs from the sandwiches and licking his chubby fingers.

"The what?" Evelyn fell back into her chair.

"Well, since you are unable to pay me half of the assets left by your father, we will have to sell everything and split it down the middle." Monroe licked his fingers again and dug more papers from his jacket pocket. "I've been to Farrington, the county seat of this fine county, and I have filed a lien on the estate and assets left by your father. A copy of your brother's expectation of inheritance has also been filed with the clerk. Since we will have to sell everything, I will ask the judge tomorrow to order the sale." Monroe made some sort of smacking sound as he ran his tongue around his mouth. Evelyn felt as though she would get sick that very moment.

"I'm sorry, Mr. Monroe. But I have no idea of how to respond to all of this right now. Would you please leave and let me contemplate this problem." Evelyn did not stand up. She was not sure her legs would hold her at that moment.

"Have it your way for now, Madame. I'll just leave you a copy of the paperwork. But know this—I will be talking to the judge tomorrow and ask him to expedite the sale." Monroe slapped the papers down on the sofa and left.

Evelyn sat in a high back wicker chair on the back veranda. Evening had fallen even though she was not aware of it. She was mesmerized by the sight of a barge quietly moving downriver—its lights twinkling in the early evening darkness. A whippoorwill joined in with the katydids to serenade her. This was her father's favorite place to sit and watch his beloved river. She missed him dearly. He had died in his sleep at the age of eighty-three two months ago. Peaceful, she thought. Which seemed fitting for the river man. He was a strong man in both body and spirit, and he always seemed at peace with himself and his world. He adored Evelyn. She could just picture him now coming onto the veranda after a long time away from home—tall, handsome and always happy to see her.

He had a difficult time when Evelyn's mother passed away years ago. He was in New Orleans and Evelyn was in Nashville at school when her mother became very ill with pneumonia. Evelyn made it home before her mother died and never left her bedside those last days, but her father did not make it home in time. He was distraught. She was the love of his life, and he felt robbed of that one last moment to hold her in his arms. Evelyn's thoughts turned to her mother—of their home when she was young. At one time four generations of Jamison's lived in the home. It was a clamorous and active home. Evelyn leaned back in her chair and closed her eyes letting herself become immersed in memories of her youth. Love, peacefulness, happiness—feelings that her memories evoked—with her mother at the center of the magic. Oh, those days of losing her mother . . . . Evelyn opened her eyes again. She was thankful that her mother was not around to witness the destruction brought about by her only son. And her father—what would he think of the current turn of events? Those days of sorrow and grief, mourning the deaths of her parents, decades apart, would have been even more difficult without Esther. How fortunate was she now to have Esther and Clovis.

Several years before her mother died and a short while before Evelyn left for school, her father was in New Orleans checking on the business and her brother at Tulane. One night he ate dinner at a small place in the French Quarter and knew that he had just eaten the best meal of his life. He just couldn't get over thinking about those savory oysters with their distinctive taste. He went back before he left for home to inquire about the cook, and Esther came out to meet him. Over the next few days he convinced Esther and her husband Clovis to come back to Tennessee with him. He built them a small cottage on the grounds. Esther cooked for the family while Clovis took care of the grounds and maintenance work. They both flourished in their new home, though they never had children. Esther always said that was okay because the Jamisons were her family to take care of. At her young age, she was already an accomplished Creole cook, but she didn't know much about Southern cooking. However, it didn't take long, under the guidance of Mrs. Jamison, for her to become a superb Southern cook. In no time at all, her biscuits and cornbread rivaled any cook in the area.

Esther was only five years older than Evelyn. She and Clovis had been with the family for over four decades, and since her father's death, Evelyn had convinced Esther and Clovis to move into the house. They took a room in the back wing behind the kitchen. It felt good to have someone else in the house with her. Yes, Evelyn thought, this was their home, too.

"Now, Miss Evelyn, you need to eat." Esther stood in the doorway holding the screen door open. "I got your supper in here keeping warm." Esther walked over to Evelyn, letting the screen door slam. Oh, that familiar sound of home, Evelyn thought. "Now ain't nothing goin' to solve itself tonight, Miss Evelyn. And it certainly not gonna make it any better with you starvin' yourself.

Now, come on now. It's getting late."

The next morning Evelyn walked into the kitchen dressed for the day with a new determination. It had been a restless night tossing and turning, trying to figure out some way out of this mess. Then towards dawn she came up with exactly what she needed to do. Nobody was going to take her home from her, and she would do whatever it took to make sure that didn't happen.

Esther gave Evelyn a look of disbelief when Evelyn set down at the kitchen table.

"Now don't look at me that way, Esther. It's just me now, and I don't see any reason to be eating in the dining room all by myself. So," Evelyn gave Esther a determined look, "I have decided to eat here in the kitchen." She got back up and went through to the dining room and collected her place setting. She returned to the kitchen and set her place at the kitchen table.

"Um, um," Esther shook her head as she turned back to the bacon cooking on the stove. "You dressed awful nice for just a regular day, Miss Evelyn. You got plans?"

"Actually, I do indeed." Evelyn picked up her coffee cup and headed for the stove.

"I'll get that for you, Miss Evelyn."

"No, I can get my own coffee." Evelyn reached for the coffee pot on the stove.

Esther laid a breakfast plate on the table still shaking her head at the thought of Miss Evelyn sitting at her kitchen table.

"Do you need Clovis to get the car out?" Esther asked.

"Yes, I'm just going down to Main Street. He can drop me off, then I'll have Maggie at the drug store call when I'm ready for him to pick me up"

"Yes'm, I'll have Clovis ready with the car just here directly."

Evelyn went upstairs after breakfast—brushed her teeth, put on her hat and gloves, and hung her pocketbook on her arm. She looked at herself in the mirror and mustered her best look of determination. She could feel her heart flutter a little and realized that she was a little nervous. She wasn't accustomed to taking care of business. Well, actually she had never taken care of business.

Lawyer Gibbons walked her though everything when her father passed away. He filed the life insurance policy with Lincoln National that her father had bought years ago from a salesman at the hotel. Then he set up her bank account so she could write checks and get cash for household needs. He even taught her how to write the checks.

But this would be different, Evelyn thought as Clovis drove her the short piece into River Bluff. She had him drop her off in front of the Jamison Hotel. Yes, the hotel was lost in the bankruptcy also, but the new owners kept the historical name. Evelyn's grandfather loved New Orleans, and commissioned the building of a hotel at the end of Main Street just above the landing. It was designed in the architectural style of the French Quarter with a second story covered balcony that wrapped around the building with its ornate ironwork and railings offering a magnificent view of the river. In its heyday, riverboats often stopped at the landing and passengers would stay the night at the charming hotel and visit the quaint little river town.

Evelyn assumed that Mr. Monroe was staying at the Jamison and hoped he wouldn't see her as Clovis helped her out of the car.

"Thank you Clovis. Now, I'll have Maggie call you when I need you to pick me up."

"She ain't there no mo', Miss Evelyn. She done gone up North somewheres."

"Oh. Well . . . I'll get someone to call you. You just go on home now."

After Clovis pulled the car away from the curb, Evelyn crossed the street and entered the River Bluff Savings and Loan. Her shoes clicked on the wood plank floors as she crossed to one of the teller windows.

"Good morning, Imogen." Evelyn began removing her gloves. "I'm here to see Mr. Conroy, please."

"I'm not sure, but I think he is busy right now. Do you have an appointment?" Imogen flipped her pencil back and forth in her fingers.

"Yes, I'm sure he is busy. And, no, I don't have an appointment. Please tell him that I'm here. I'm sure that he will see me." Evelyn felt her heart flutter again and it was getting difficult to breath. *Don't let them see my nervousness*, she thought. *Remember, determination and confidence.* Imogen huffed and left her window for a moment.

"Miss Evelyn, it's so nice to see you," J. D. Conroy said a moment later as he opened the side door to his office. "Please come in, and let's see what we can do for you." Evelyn picked up her gloves and entered Conroy's office. She took a seat in front of his desk as he moved around the desk and sat down. The office was very cold and dark due to the pulled curtains. Heavy cigarette smoke hung in the air and the hum of the window air-conditioner sounded strained as it worked to pump even more coldness into the room. Evelyn opened her pocketbook to stall for time. Conroy leaned forward in expectation. She dropped her gloves in the pocketbook and snapped it closed. Conroy sat back a little disappointed. "Miss Evelyn, I'm so sorry to hear of your father's passing. But I think Lawyer Gibbons has everything set up for you."

"Thank you, and yes everything is running nicely. I'm also so sorry to hear of your son's death, Mr. Conroy." Evelyn looked down at her hands sitting on top of her pocketbook.

"Thank you. It has been especially hard on his mother." They sat in silence for a moment. "What can I do for you today, Miss Evelyn?"

"Mr. Conroy, I have come today to mortgage all of my property," Evelyn gushed out in a flurry. Conroy placed his elbows on his desk and put his chin on his interlocked hands. He looked down for a moment. Then he reared back in his chair and let out a great howl of laughter.

"What in the world . . ." Conroy managed to spit out between laughter.

"Well, for heaven's sake, Mr. Conroy." Evelyn could feel redness spreading over her face and neck. "I don't see what's so funny."

"Miss Evelyn," Conroy said as he managed to gain some composure, "a mortgage is a loan."

"Yes," Evelyn said.

"Well the word loan implies that it will be paid back."

"Yes?" was all Evelyn could say.

"Miss Evelyn, you don't have an income that would allow you to make payments on a mortgage. You only have your father's life insurance money, and what little he had in savings at his death, to live on."

"Well," Evelyn stammered.

"Now if you need to cut back in order to make things last, you may want to consider selling out. The money you make from the sale and the money you have in the bank could possibly get you through. I'm sure you could find nice accommodations in an elderly ladies boarding home."

"I do not plan to sell my family's home, Mr. Conroy. And, I assure you that I'm not ready for some old ladies' home."

"Well, you could begin by letting those uppity coloreds you have working for you go. That would save you some." Conroy lit a cigarette and looked amused with himself. Evelyn opened her pocketbook and reached for her handkerchief. She was feeling faint again.

"But," Evelyn whispered as she blotted her face.

"But nothing, Miss Evelyn," Conroy interrupted. "Now you have assets, yes, but none of it is liquid." At that point Evelyn wasn't even sure if he was speaking English. She dropped her handkerchief into her pocketbook and took out her gloves.

"What are you needing all that much money for anyway?"

"Thank you for your time, Mr. Conroy." Evelyn rose hoping that her legs would support her.

"Good bye, Miss Evelyn." She could hear him laughing again as she left the room.

Evelyn stepped out on the sidewalk not sure if she could convey herself very far. The humiliation of it all stung—no, she wouldn't cry. The heat was even more oppressive than usual since she had just stepped out of a refrigerator. She walked up the sidewalk towards the river and spotted a bench outside the River Cafe. Sitting under the covered sidewalk, it would be a good place to relax a bit in the shade. As she walked in front of the cafe, she noticed several people sitting at tables, and one of them was Lawyer Gibbons. She tried to no avail to get his attention by waving her handkerchief. Totally discouraged she fell onto the bench to rest.

"Young man, young man," Evelyn called after a young colored

boy walking down the sidewalk.

"Me?" the boy asked.

"Yes, you. Please go into the cafe and ask Lawyer Gibbons to come out and see me," Evelyn instructed, trying to catch her breath.

"Me?" the boy repeated.

"Yes, of course you. There's no one else here." She opened her purse and brought out a stick of gum. "Here's you a stick of gum to express my thanks." She held out the gum.

"I can't go in there."

"Well, for heaven's sake! I certainly can't go in there." Evelyn held out the gum again. "Now don't be rude and do as I ask."

"I'll get in a whole heap of trouble if'n I goes in there. Anyways, why can't you go in there?" he asked.

"Well," Evelyn looked around. "I just can't that's all!" She hesitated.

"They won't let you in like they won't let me in?" he asked. He looked at her kind of funny. "You do something wrong?"

"No, certainly not," she scoffed. "It's a river cafe," she whispered.

"What's wrong with that?" he asked.

"Oh, I declare!" Evelyn said in exasperation realizing that she had been talking to this boy far too long. "Here, now take this stick of gum and go tell Lawyer Gibbons that I need to see him right now."

The boy took the gum and turned towards the cafe. He cupped his hands and looked through the window. He moved up the sidewalk, stopped and looked through the window again. Then he went up to the door and knocked on the glass. After a moment, he knocked again and motioned for someone inside to come out. Anna Grace Merriman opened the door and looked down at the boy.

"What's wrong?" she asked. "Are you okay?"

"That lady there needs to see Lawyer Gibbons right now she say," the boy answered pointing at Evelyn.

Anna Grace walked over to the bench as Evelyn turned her chin to the river as if she were not aware of what was going on.

"Miss Evelyn, is that you?" Anna Grace asked as she

approached the bench. "Are you okay?"

"Oh, yes, dear. I'm just fine. Just enjoying this fine weather and the view of the river." Anna Grace sat down beside Evelyn.

"The boy says that you need to see Lawyer Gibbons. He's just right inside."

"Thanks for the gum, lady," the boy yelled from down the sidewalk. Anna Grace giggled. Evelyn was horrified as she watched the boy skip off.

"Yes, if he happens to be here, that would be nice," Evelyn said turning back to Anna Grace.

"Why don't you come on in, Miss Evelyn. He won't mind, and my aunts would love to have you," Anna Grace stood offering her hand to Evelyn.

"Oh, no, dear. I think I'll just stay here. It's comfortable here."

"Well, okay. I'll go tell Lawyer Gibbons that you're here."

Gibbons came out the door several moments later with his paper napkin still stuffed into his collar. He pulled off the napkin and wiped his mouth as he approached Evelyn.

"Hello, Miss Evelyn. It's nice to see you," he said as he sat down beside her. "Is everything alright? Can I do something for you?" he asked.

"No, everything is not alright," she felt tears welling up. She took a deep breath and thought, *determination and confidence*!

"Why don't you come on inside and join me at my table. Would you like something to eat?"

"Oh, I couldn't," Evelyn replied.

"Now, Miss Evelyn," Gibbons said, catching on to what was going on, "it's a nice place. I eat here all the time and you know Edna and Sally Bratcher." Evelyn was ignoring him gazing down at the river. "At least come in and have a glass of water. It's awful hot out here," Gibbons said.

"Oh, for heaven's sake, alright. A glass of water would be nice right now." Gibbons offered his hand and she was grateful for it.

Evelyn stepped into the cafe, and if it hadn't been for Gibbons at her side, she would have immediately turned and left. The cafe was about half full with the end of the lunch crowd—mostly men with some women factory workers scattered around. Gibbons held her seat for her and she considered whether or not to take off her gloves.

"They're staring at me," she whispered to Gibbons.

He leaned forward and whispered, "No, they're staring at me wondering what someone like me is doing with such a lovely lady at my table." He leaned back and smiled at her. She was unable to return his smile. "Now, as you can see I have just been served my pie, so why don't you join me and have a piece of this wonderful pie."

"Oh, no, I couldn't," Evelyn said. She decided not to remove her gloves after all.

"It would be my pleasure, ma'am if you would join me. I assure you it's delicious." Gibbons folded the newspaper he had been reading and placed it on one of the empty chairs. "Maybe some lunch. Have you eaten? I bet you would love their catfish—maybe with some white beans, fried okra, and cornbread that will melt in your mouth."

Evelyn sat with her gloved hands resting on her pocketbook, not wanting to touch the table. Anna Grace came over to take her order. "Just a glass of water, dear. Thank you." Gibbons smiled and began eating his pie.

"Evelyn," he said when he had finished about half of his pie. "Why don't you walk back to my office with me, and we'll talk about what's on your mind?" Gibbons asked as he folded his napkin and placed it on the table. Evelyn was amazed at how quickly everything flooded back into her mind.

"Yes, I would like that, if you have the time."

"Oh, Esther, what can I do? We are getting ready to lose everything. And, I mean everything," Evelyn lamented as she sat at the kitchen table with her head buried in her hands. "Lawyer Gibbons says that I have no recourse at all with the mess my brother has gotten me into."

After Evelyn had disclosed the whole situation that her brother had left her in, Gibbons had given her a ride home and looked over the paperwork. He just sat there on the sofa reading for the longest time as Evelyn sat in her chair twisting her handkerchief. Finally, he laid the papers down on the table and grimly looked up at

Evelyn.

"Well, it seems that Joe has struck again," Gibbons spoke. "He seems bound and determined to take it all. Evelyn, I just don't see any way out of this. Monroe has the right to demand sale of real and personal property. It is the same as if your brother came to town after your father's death and demanded his half of the estate. Instead, he couldn't wait, so he signed over his portion to someone else. Cashed out early, if you will." Gibbons leaned back into the sofa. His heart was breaking for this woman who had done nothing in her life except suffer the consequences of her brother's actions. "Do you have any information as to the whereabouts of your brother?" he asked.

"No, just what Monroe has told me. He tried to track him down, and all he could find out was that Joe is out west somewhere—maybe Arizona." Evelyn dropped her head and watched her hands straighten out her handkerchief, smoothing it out to all corners, smoothing out the wrinkles, straightening the lace border, pressing it to her lap.

"I'm so sorry, Evelyn," Gibbons spoke with a heavy heart. "But, I don't see any paperwork indicating that a lien has been filed with the court. Is that what he told you?"

"Yes, he said that he had been to Farrington and filed a lien with the clerk."

"Well, I'll call the courthouse tomorrow and check on that. In the meantime, I'm sorry to say, the expectancy of inheritance looks legitimate."

"Thank you. Well, I suppose that's that," she said as she stood. "Will I be able to choose any personal items to keep, or does it all go on the auction block?"

"Make a list of things that are dear to you, and I'll see what I can negotiate with Monroe," Gibbons said as he put on his hat. "Evelyn, stay in close contact with me, and I'll walk you through all of this. I'm here for you any time of day."

"So there you have it," Evelyn said after she had explained the whole situation to Esther. "We are getting ready to lose everything. I suppose you and Clovis might want to go back to New Orleans?"

"New Orleans?" Esther grunted as she turn from the stove that was simmering away with supper. "Miss Evelyn, this here is our home. We have been here for some forty years. I may have been born there, and I may still have Creole running through my blood, but *this* is our home. We'll be with you no matter where you land, Miss Evelyn. You can count on that. You stuck with us!" Esther laughed, and Evelyn gave a weak smile.

"As I see it, Miss Evelyn, it is time to protect our home." Esther turned her attention back to her cooking—stirring the beans for a moment, checking on the cornbread. "I been thinking," she said pointing a spoon in Evelyn's direction. "You need to invite that Monroe feller to supper tomorrow night."

"What? I'll do no such thing!"

"Now, think about it. You could ask't him to put off the sale for just a bit in order to give you more time to see if'n you can come up with the money. We'll feed him out on the back veranda. You can show off how lovely the home is and how much you love it."

"But I'll never be able to come up with that kind of money," Evelyn moaned. "I've tried everything I can think of today. Even subjecting myself to the humiliation of asking J. D. Conroy for money." Evelyn paused to catch her breath as the horrifying events of the day came to mind.

"Now, listen. I'll have Clovis take me down to the groc'ry sto' and I'll pick out a nice roast and some fresh beans, corn, and some potatoes. I'll make up some gravy—have Clovis go down to the cellar and open up one of your Daddy's fine bottles of wine. I'll serve a good ole buttermilk pie with coffee for dessert." Esther paused for a moment. "Now, Miss Evelyn, you just leave everything to me and Clovis. We take care of everything for you."

"Oh, I don't know Esther. I don't think I can spend another moment with that boorish man. He's just horrible!"

"You go on in there and write a note to him inviting him to supper. Oh, and tell him it will be a late supper, around eight o'clock, so as he can sit on the veranda and watch the sunset over the river. See the lights from the river as he eats his dessert. Clovis will take the note to the hotel, and then we'll take care of everything from there. Just don't you worry none about anything a'tall."

"Well, I suppose it's worth a try. But, I don't think he's

interested in anything but money," Evelyn said as she left for the parlor.

"Maybe it's a barge," Anna Grace said.

"Nope, them ain't barge lights." Mary Nell leaned forward to get a better look out the window.

"It's just cars getting off the ferry," Anna Grace speculated as she strained to see better through the early morning fog. It was still very early and the Tennessee River Cafe had not opened for breakfast yet. Anna Grace and Mary Nell had about half the chairs down when they noticed some activity going on down at the ferry landing.

"No, som'pin's goin' on down thar." Mary Nell looked at Anna Grace, excitement gleaming in her eyes. She turned back to the window. "Look thar goes Oscar Treadway running down to see." She grabbed Anna Grace by the arm. "Let's go see!"

"Let's go! Aunt Ed," Anna Grace yelled back to the kitchen. "We're going down to the ferry to see what's going on." The girls ran to the door. Anna Grace unlocked the door and opened it just as Aunt Sally was coming out of the kitchen.

"You girls aren't going anywhere. We'll be opening soon. Come back here and finish these chairs," Aunt Sally called after the girls, wiping her hands on her apron. Anna Grace locked the door back from the outside, and the girls giggled as they ran off toward the landing.

Dawn was just arriving at the river town. It was that moment between dark and light. The fog lay heavy across the river. Anna Grace could just make out dark figures moving in the fog backlit by the lights. As they crossed the road, Deputy Mankin pulled up in his patrol car.

"Oh, goodness," Anna Grace said. "There must have been some kind of accident. Let's see if we can get closer." She pulled on Mary Nell's arm. The girls made their way down to where a small crowd had gathered around John Morgan's fishing boat.

"Who is he?" "What happened?" "Is he dead?" were the questions that were floating around the crowd.

"Let me get through here," Deputy Mankin said as he moved

through the gathering. "Let's see what we've got here."

Anna Grace could get a good view now, and she grabbed Mary Nell's arm tight when she realized that John Morgan and another man were dragging a man's body from the water. They laid him in the grass beside the water's edge. Deputy Mankin put his hands on his hips, resting them on top of his holster belt as he looked down on the body.

"I found him down river some just at the bottom of Jamison's Bluff," John Morgan explained. "I wasn't sure what it was at first. Then I was able to get a good light on it, and that's when I realized that I was looking at a man's face. I don't mind tellin' ya that it was a spooky sight to behold. He's so big that it took a good bit of maneuvering to get him off the rocks. Then I couldn't get him over into the boat by myself. So, I put my tow rope around him, under his arms, and pulled him up to the side of the boat, and brought him on in that way. I know that's not very befittin' a dead man, but I didn't know what else to do."

Anna Grace pushed in a little closer. "Oh goodness, that's the man that comes in the cafe all the time."

"You know who he is, Anna Grace?" asked Deputy Mankin.

" Yeah, he's staying over at the Jamison. He's been in town about a week."

"Do you know his name?" Mankin asked.

"Um, let's see. Oh yeah, it's Monroe. Mr. Monroe." She thought for a minute. "I think he's from Memphis. That's what he told me, Memphis. Oh, this is so terrible. I've never seen a dead man before. Well, you know, not in a funeral home."

"Monroe, uh. Morgan, can you stay with the body for just a little longer? I'll call the ambulance to come pick him up, and then go up to the hotel to see what they know about him."

"Miss Evelyn, Dep'ty Mankin's here to see you," Esther announced.

"Goodness me, why in the world would he need to see me?" Evelyn stood up from her seat on the back veranda where she was reading the newspaper.

"Didn't say. I showed him into the parlor."

Deputy Mankin removed his hat as Evelyn entered the parlor. "Miss Evelyn. How are you today?"

"I'm fine Deputy. Just enjoying the morning on the back veranda. It's cool out there this morning. Would you like to join me there and have some coffee?"

"Yes, that sounds nice, thank you." He followed Evelyn out back. After he had walked around the veranda for a moment admiring the view of the river, he sat down as Esther brought out his coffee. "Miss Evelyn, do you know a man named Charlie Monroe?" he asked as he lifted his cup and blew on the coffee.

"Why yes, I do. What makes you ask about him?" Evelyn stirred her coffee that Esther had freshened for her.

"Has he been here to see you?"

"Yes, on two different occasions. He said he was staying up at the hotel. He's from Memphis."

"Was he here last night by any chance?" Mankin asked.

"Yes," Evelyn looked surprised. "As a matter of fact he was. I invited him to supper last night. We enjoyed supper and dessert right here on this veranda." Evelyn looked questioningly at the deputy. Mankin returned his cup to the saucer.

"I'm sorry to have to tell you this, Miss Evelyn, but Charlie Monroe was found dead this morning on the rocks below your house. John Morgan found him at the bottom of that bluff right there." Mankin watched her closely.

"Mercy me! I just can't believe it. He was here just last night. Deputy, I can't tell you how distraught I am by this news. Thank you, though, for coming to tell me about it." Evelyn looked out toward the river. "I just can't imagine how that happened."

"Yes, neither can I." Mankin looked around for a moment. "Did you see or hear anything last night after your guest left?"

"No, nothing. But I'll tell you, I went straight up to bed as he was leaving. Yesterday was an exhausting day for me."

"Miss Evelyn, I need to ask you about something else. When I searched his room at the hotel, I found some legal papers. They are papers signed by your brother, Joe—an expectancy of inheritance signed over to Monroe.

"I see." Evelyn looked down at her hands in her lap. "Well, then you know the cause of his visits. Why he came here from

Memphis."

"Yes, ma'am, I do. And I hate to say it, but it does seem suspicious that he ended up dead at the base of your bluff."

"Deputy Mankin!" Evelyn gasped. "Are you suggesting . . . " Evelyn stammered. "Are you saying that I had something to do with his death?" Evelyn said incredulously.

"Well, no, Miss Evelyn. But . . . "

"I would certainly hope not, Deputy."

"But you've got to admit that you do benefit from his death. And you are the reason he came to River Bluff." Mankin started to continue. "And . . . "

"And nothing. I assure you that I had nothing to do with that man's demise. And that sir, is the end of that." Evelyn folded her hands in her lap and held her head high. "Besides the lien against the property is already filed," she huffed.

"Lien? I didn't find any evidence of a lien being filed in his room. I'll call up to Farrington and see if it's been filed." Mankin took another sip of coffee. "I'll need to talk to Clovis and Esther, Miss Evelyn."

"That's fine, I'm sure. I can't think that they will tell you any different than what I've already told you."

"I also need to notify the next of kin. Monroe didn't by any chance say anything about his family did he?"

"As a matter of fact he did. Just last night—I was just making polite conversation. Truth be told, that man is, was, a pompous, arrogant, boorish man. Anyway, I was just trying to carry on a polite conversation. He told me that he never married, and that his parents have passed away. He had a younger brother but he was killed in the war."

"Did he tell you anything about what he does in Memphis?"

"Yes, he said he owned a night club, and that it had a back room for gambling card playing men. That, of course, is how he met my brother." Evelyn gave a disgusted turn of the nose. "Truth be known, Deputy Mankin, he was not a very nice man. He was terribly rude."

"Miss Evelyn, I need to talk with Esther and Clovis."

"Yes, of course. I think I saw Clovis come in earlier. He's probably in the kitchen with Esther. I'll get them." Evelyn returned with Esther and Clovis slowly following behind her. Evelyn sat down while the two stood in front of the table.

"Clovis, Esther. I just have a few questions for you about Charlie Monroe—the man that ate supper here last night. He was found dead at the base of Jamison's Bluff this morning."

"Oh my heavens," Esther gasped.

"Could you tell me when was the last time that either of you saw him?" Mankin continued.

"Well sir, just a little after I served dessert, Miss Evelyn came into the kitchen and said that she goin' up to bed. She looked very worried and tired. She ask't me to show Mr. Monroe out. I had just given Clovis his dinner at the kitchen table, and just took a minute to pour his coffee. By the time I got out to the back veranda, Mr. Monroe, he was done gone. I just figured he went around the house to leave. That's the last we knew of Mr. Monroe," Esther finished.

"And do you agree with this statement, Clovis?" Mankin asked.

"Yesuh, that be the way it was." Clovis put his hand at the small of Esther's back. Evelyn noticed that Esther was shaking and thought it odd.

"Well, thank you. That's all I need for now. If I think of more, I'll come back. Thank you for the coffee, Miss Evelyn. I'll let myself out." Mankin opened the screen door and paused. "Clovis can you think of any explanation as to how the man ended up at the bottom of that bluff?" he asked.

"No suh, I been thinkin' on that just now. I reckon he just got turned around. Maybe thought he was on the front porch or som'pin." Clovis thought for a minute. "Now, the gentleman did drink an awful lot of Mista Jamison's wine."

"Hmm." Mankin turned his hat around in his hands. "Well, I'll be going." He let the screen door slam as he went into the house.

Esther seemed to melt into the floor.

"Esther! Are you okay?" Evelyn jumped up and went to her side. Clovis was holding her up.

"She be awright, Miss Evelyn. She just feeling a bit down today," Clovis said. "I'll just get her into the kitchen, and she be just fine." Clovis led Esther into the house.

"Does she need to see the doctor?" Evelyn called after them.

"No'ma'am. She be just fine. You'll see." Clovis called back to her as he entered the house with his wife.

"Esther, I have come up with the most brilliant idea," Evelyn announced as she came into the kitchen about a week later after an especially fitful night of little sleep.

Deputy Mankin had called the afternoon before to tell Evelyn that he and the coroner had come to the conclusion that Monroe's death was accidental. He also told Evelyn that he agreed with Lawyer Gibbons that Monroe had not filed a lien against her property. "I guess he was just using that as a threat to strong-arm you into coming up with the money. He'd probably rather you did that than have to go through the trouble of a sale," Deputy Mankin had explained.

"Oh, Esther just wait 'til I tell you all about it! Good morning, Clovis." Clovis was finishing his breakfast at the kitchen table.

"I jus' be a'leavin', Miss Evelyn." Clovis moved to get up.

"No, Clovis, stay. I want you to hear this, too." Evelyn took a seat at the table. Clovis looked over at Esther expressing his discomfort with a glance. Esther signaled for him to stay seated, and brought Evelyn some coffee. "Oh, Esther and Clovis, I have just a marvelous idea. Here, sit Esther." Esther shrugged her shoulders since it seemed that all decorum had gone completely out the door, and sat down at the table with her coffee. "I have decided to sell the house and the land down river and move to Nashville!" Esther's eyebrows shot up as she looked at Clovis. Her face seemed to lose all color.

"But, Miss Evelyn," Clovis stammered.

"I've been trying, ever since all this started, to adjust to the idea of having to sell the house to satisfy my brother's debt. And I tried to think of where I would go—what would I do? But splitting the proceeds with Mr. Monroe wouldn't have left me with enough to do much. Well now that all that nasty business is over, I started thinking, why not sell?" Esther looked as if she might just fall out of her chair. She held onto Clovis' arm for support.

"Oh, Esther, now don't look like that. It will be wonderful. Life is nothing but a series of letting go. And I have let go of everything—my trip to Paris, a chance for a wonderful life as a rich debutante, all of my dreams, gone. I've let go of my mother, my father, and now—now I'm going to let go of this house and this town that has me trapped here."

"Oh, Lordy, I just can't believe this!" Esther fanned herself with a kitchen towel. Clovis looked as if he didn't know what to say. He just patted Esther's hand.

"I tell you those years that I spent in Nashville were the most wonderful times of my life. I don't know why I haven't thought of this sooner. Well, I guess I couldn't have with Daddy to take care of and all. But, now! For the first time in my life I'm free. Free as a bird I tell you! Sorry, I just feel down right giddy. I am not an old woman. I'm not but sixty years old, and by George, I have some good years left in me. In Nashville there are all kinds of great society—wonderful people, churches, shopping.

"Oh, Esther, it will be so much fun. We can go through the house and pick out what we want to take with us. Then sell or store the rest. Sell everything I say! We'll take the money and buy a lovely home in Nashville. It's just beautiful there. You'll love it!" Evelyn was talking so fast that she hadn't noticed the looks going on between Clovis and Esther. She looked at Esther who seemed simply horrified.

"Esther, what's wrong with you. Now listen, don't you worry. You'll just love Nashville!"

"But, Miss Evelyn. We done went through so much trouble to save the house, and now you wants to sell?"

"Oh goodness, we didn't go to that much trouble. Now listen, I'm going right down to Lawyer Gibbons to get things rolling. Clovis, I'm going to have some breakfast, and then I want you to drive me down to Lawyer Gibbons' office. I want to get things started right away."

Evelyn sashayed into Lawyer Gibbons' office just so full of herself. Excitement emanated from her as she made a beeline for his office right past the empty secretary's desk. She barged right into the office. Betty Jane Pinkerton, Lawyer Gibbons' secretary, was sitting opposite his desk taking dictation. Gibbons stood as Evelyn walked in the door.

"Mr. Gibbons, I'm so sorry about this unscheduled intrusion, but I have the best news. I just couldn't wait to discuss it with you. Betty Jane, it's nice to see you." Evelyn plopped down in the other chair facing Gibbons' desk.

"Evelyn, this is a pleasant surprise. Betty Jane, we'll finish this up later." Gibbons was amused by this sudden appearance of Evelyn. It was totally out of character for her. "Miss Evelyn, what brings you here today. You look as if you've had some good news."

"No, not good news. It's a brilliant idea that has me so excited."

"Well, please, I'm intrigued to know what's going on." He sat back in his chair and laced his fingers together across his belly.

"I have decided to sell. Sell everything! I'm here for you to get the ball rolling. I don't want to wait any longer than I have to."

"But, Miss Evelyn . . . "

"Now, I know," Evelyn cut him off. "I know that you must think me quite fickle since not long ago I sat in this very chair distraught by the idea of losing my home to that Monroe fellow. But, you see, that whole situation got me to thinking. I tried to come up with what I would do if I really did lose the house. Well, first off, you know how much I loved being in Nashville the few years that I was there for school. What a wonderful time that was." Gibbons opened his mouth to speak, but Evelyn went on. "Anyway, now that things are concluded with that nasty Monroe business, I have decided to sell everything and buy a lovely home in Nashville." She sat on the edge of her chair. "Live a little! I'm not over the hill yet, you know. I just think it will be so exciting. Oh, and Esther and Clovis are coming with me. They seem so shocked at the idea, but I know they will come to love it once we are there." Evelyn took a breath.

"I guess I have been talking a mile a minute," she continued without giving Gibbons a chance to interject. "But now that Daddy has passed on—well, you know—before, I had never stopped to think about what I was going to do with myself. And now I have, and it's all so exhilarating! I just might take that trip to Paris that I planned so many years ago."

Gibbons hardly knew what to say. "But, Evelyn, do you think

that you may regret selling your family home?"

"No, I'm ready to let it go. I've been trapped there for so long. I feel so free now, like a door has been opened just for me!" Gibbons could see the exuberance radiating from her. It just broke his heart.

"Nashville has changed a lot since you were last there. You may not like the big city atmosphere anymore," he added gently.

"Oh, and when I was there, I used to go down Broad to Christ Church Episcopal for church. What a lovely church, and such wonderful people." Evelyn was still dreaming of her wonderful future. Her eyes sparkled. "And such wonderful society what with garden parties and church socials. Shopping! I'll need some new clothes and shoes." Evelyn really noticed Gibbons' expression for the first time. "What is wrong with you, Mr. Gibbons? Aren't you excited for me?"

"I'm so sorry, Evelyn." Gibbons sighed heavily. Evelyn eyed her attorney, her friend, and noticed lines of tension around his mouth. She saw pain in his eyes. Finally, she looked down at her folded hands in her lap and waited.

"Evelyn, you can't sell your home." He leaned forward supporting himself on his desk, frowning. "Now, it is true that your father's estate is free and clear, no encumbrances, no liens. And that debt, should it turn up at a later point, which I doubt it will since Monroe does not have any family, that is Joe's debt. His problem." Gibbons looked closely at Evelyn. "Now I'm sure that Joe never intended for things to get this far with Monroe. He probably thought that he would make lots of money selling cotton and pay him back." He paused for Evelyn to keep up with him. "But, either way, the home itself and the extra property is part of you father's estate, and half of that estate is owned by your brother."

"But, it's my home!" Anger flew all over her. "Other than a few visits, Joe has not returned to that house since he left for college. I'm the one that took care of my mother—watched over my father. It's *my* home. I have lived in that place my whole life with exception of the few years that I spent in Nashville." Evelyn retrieved her handkerchief from her purse.

"I'm sorry to say," Gibbons said quietly, "that the only way that you can sell is to locate Joe. And then half of the proceeds would go to him, unless he were to sign the property over to you. But, I don't see him doing that." They sat in silence for a good amount of time. Gibbons patiently waited for her to process the change of plans. He didn't move. He didn't want to distract her thoughts.

"Well." Evelyn tried to speak after some time had passed. She fiddled with her handkerchief some more. "I suppose there's nothing left but to just sit up on that bluff and watch the river go by."

Evelyn walked into the house a different woman. Esther thought she looked as though she had aged ten years in the little bit of time that she had been gone.

"Miss Evelyn, goodness gracious, what's happened?" Esther asked as she went to Evelyn. "You aw'right? Let me get a cool cloth to put on your forehead."

"Just fix me a glass of tea and bring it out to the veranda."

"Yes'm. You just come on here and let me help you. You home now." Esther followed Evelyn down the hall, crooning softly: "You just rest . . . You home now . . . Ain't nobody gonna take it away. Don't you worry . . . Esther and Clovis, we see to that."

Evelyn kept walking, in a daze, straight out the back screen door and onto the veranda. She sat in her father's favorite chair . . . and watched the river go by.